"I didn't see that," Carter repeated over and over. "I did *not* see that."

"It's not scientifically possible," Angelo muttered, squeezing his monster notebook until his fingers turned white.

"It has to be some kind of trick," Dana agreed. "Like in those haunted houses you see at Halloween. Or a movie effect of some kind."

Angie was standing with her hands on her knees, panting. "Whatever it was, at least we got away. We're all safe."

Nick looked around, taking a quick count, and his gut clenched in a hot ball of fear. "Not all of us," he whispered. "Cody's gone."

Library of Congress Cataloging-in-Publication Data
Savage, J. Scott (Jeffrey Scott), 1963-
  Making the team / J. Scott Savage. — First edition.
    pages cm. — (Case file #13 ; #2)
  Summary: A mysterious private school has opened in town and
Nick, Carter, and Angelo join forces with their rivals Angie, Tiffany,
and Dana to uncover the mystery behind the school's inhumanly
good football team.
  ISBN 978-0-06-213335-9 (pbk.)
  [1. Monsters—Fiction. 2. Video recordings—Production and
direction—Fiction. 3. Best friends—Fiction. 4. Friendship—Fiction.
5. Football—Fiction. 6. Scientists—Fiction. 7. Supernatural—
Fiction.] I. Title.
PZ7.S25897Mak 2013   2013021851
[Fic]—dc23   CIP
                                                              AC

Typography by Sarah Nichole Kaufman
18 19 20   BRR 10 9 8 7 6 5 4 3 2
❖
First paperback edition, 2014

MAKING THE TEAM

J. SCOTT SAVAGE

HARPER

An Imprint of HarperCollinsPublishers

Here
We Are
Once More

Back again? Ready for another tale so terrifying it might keep you up at night, afraid to look in your closet or under your bed? Your timing couldn't be better. Much as I feared, things are changing in Pleasant Hill. Oh, the Zombie King seems to be gone—at least for now. But something even more dangerous has arrived in his place. I suspect that Nick and his friends are going to need every shred of monster knowledge they possess—and perhaps even the help of another group of monster hunters every bit as determined as they are.

For you see, dark forces have been stirring in the last few days. Forces I haven't witnessed in nearly two hundred years. How could I have seen things that long ago, you ask? Let's just say librarians have rather lengthy life spans.

But be not distracted. Old powers are returning, and long-dead sciences are rising from their graves . . . as it were. I'm afraid I need to do some investigating on my own. I hope the boys will be all right while I'm gone. I'm sure they wouldn't do anything foolish—or danger-ous—while I'm away. Keep an eye on them, won't you? And take good notes. They may just end up in Case File 13.

CHAPTER 1

AND . . . ACTION

Nick reached the top of Dinosaur Hill and searched the deserted park. "Mr. Fitzpatrick?" he called. Wind blew through the gnarled branches of an oak that had to be at least a hundred years old. But the man he was supposed to meet was nowhere in sight. He shifted uncomfortably in his too large suit coat, clutched his briefcase, and shined his flashlight into the darkness.

From the distance came a *hoo-hoo* that sounded like a kid doing a really bad owl imitation. Nick grimaced and swung his flashlight left and right. "Something's wrong," he muttered to himself. "There's no way Fitzpatrick would miss this meeting. Unless . . ." He looked up at the night sky, where a thick bank of clouds had just cleared away. "Full moon."

Something moved through the tall grass to his right and Nick spun around—mouth dropping open. "No!" he screamed as a large gray creature with matted fur and a long pink tail leaped out of the grass and attacked him. Raising his briefcase, he managed to hit the creature in the head with a surprisingly loud *clonk!*

The creature hissed, baring its long yellow fangs.

"Fitzpatrick, is that you?" Nick asked, circling to keep the beast in front of him.

The monster bared its teeth again, red eyes flaring, and swiped Nick with its dirt-crusted claws.

Nick clutched at his chest and blood squeezed between his fingers. "Wererat," he gasped. "Must . . . get . . . serum." He snapped open his briefcase and reached for a syringe filled with a liquid that looked a little like grape Kool-Aid. Before he could reach it, the wererat was on him, scratching, biting, and even throwing a punch with one of its paws.

"Ow!" Nick yelled as the wererat's paw connected with his left ear. "That hurt."

"It serves you right for hitting me with the brief-case," the giant rat shouted back.

"That was for making the stupid owl noise," Nick

said. "It sounded totally fake."

"Cut!" Angelo stepped out from behind his tripod and turned off his video camera. He put his hands on his hips and shook his head. "If you two keep ruining every scene, we're never going to get this movie finished in time for the contest."

Carter pulled off his rat head. His face was sweaty and his bright red hair was matted to his scalp from the rubber of the mask. He pulled the plastic fangs out of his mouth. "I *like* the owl. It makes the scene more creepy."

"It makes the scene more *lame*," Nick said. He turned to Angelo. "Tell him he sounded like a kid trying to hoot."

"Maybe we could edit in a real owl," Angelo suggested. He flipped open his monster notebook and scribbled a reminder to himself.

Carter tugged at the thick gray mittens the boys had changed into rat paws. "Are you sure we have to do the whole giant rat thing? A werewolf or a killer lizard would be so much cooler."

"And done about a thousand times." Nick snorted. "Dude, we've been over this. It's a tribute to *The Princess Bride*."

"An *homage*," Angelo added—never afraid to use big words. "To the *Rodents of Unusual Size* from the fire swamp."

"I know that." Carter fanned himself and began removing the pieces of his costume. "It's just that Nick gets to be Mr. Fraley, the hero. And you get to be the director. But in the credits I'm only listed as *Wererat*. It's totally unfair."

"You're also Mr. Fitzpatrick, Larry the mad butcher, and girl in haunted house with toilet plunger," Angelo said. "That's more parts than anyone else."

Carter rolled his eyes. "A mad scientist, a guy who sells infected sausage, a rat, and a girl. *Woo-hoo.*"

"Well, time to call it a night," Angelo said. He unscrewed his camera from the tripod and packed it carefully in its case. "Have you given any more thought to how we are going to tie our film into the contest?"

"As a matter of fact, I have," Nick said. The theme of the young authors and artists contest for this year was Building a Brighter Tomorrow. Kids from fifth through twelfth grades were supposed to write an essay, paint a picture, or film a movie about how they could make the world a better place. All three of the boys thought making a movie would be awesome. But the idea of doing something about cleaning up the environment or

4

stopping war sounded totally boring.

Instead, since they all loved monsters more than anything, they'd decided to make a movie about a kindly veterinarian who eats a bunch of sausage infected with saliva from a mutant rat and turns into a killer rodent. They made the rat costume out of a bunch of old gray shag carpeting Carter's parents had in their garage, and came up with an awesome script that had lots of action and a super-disgusting scene where the rat eats all the cats in the neighborhood. The only problem was how to make their movie fit the theme of the contest.

"Okay, get this," Nick said, as they picked up the rest of their props. "After Fitzpatrick realizes he's been changing into a wererat every time it's a full moon, he gets together with the mad butcher—who it turns out used to work for a big drug company before he got fired for experimenting on the ladies in the cafeteria."

"I like it," Carter said.

Angelo tapped his notebook against his leg. "But Carter plays both the butcher and Mr. Fitzpatrick. How are we going to film him doing both parts at once?"

Nick scrunched up his mouth. "Good point. Okay, forget that. We'll have Mr. Fraley be the guy who worked at the drug company."

"There go *my* lines," Carter said.

Angelo slung his camera case over his shoulder, and the boys began walking carefully down the trail in the dark. "What does any of this have to do with building a brighter tomorrow?"

"That's what I was getting to," Nick said. "So Fitzpatrick and Fraley realize there is no hope for curing Fitzpatrick. He gets shot in the next scene anyway. But in *trying* to find a cure for the wererat, they come up with a cure for, like, all the worst diseases, making a brighter tomorrow. It's classic."

"I get shot?" Carter wailed.

"Yeah," Nick said. "But at the end of the movie, you see all these people getting cured of their diseases and the label of the medicine is called *FitzRatia*. You know, in honor of Fitzpatrick and the rat."

"Cool," Carter said. "Is there any chance I could get a medal from the president? Since I died for the cause?"

Angelo looked dubious. "That seems like a pretty weak tie-in. Don't you think the judges will realize we just added the ending for the contest?"

"Good point," Nick said. "Maybe we could—"

"Shhh," Carter held up a hand and ducked. "Everybody down."

Nick and Angelo squatted beside him. "What is it?"

Carter pointed to where the trail they were following

6

met the Dinosaur Hill parking lot. It took Nick's eyes a moment to adjust, but when they did, he spotted the hulking figure Carter had already seen.

"Frankenstein," Angelo whispered. Cody Gills, known to most of the kids at Pleasant Hill Elementary as Frankenstein, was at least twice as big as any other kid in the school. For years he'd terrorized the other kids—especially Nick, Carter, and Angelo. He'd gone out of his way to find the three of them and beat them up. But ever since they'd tricked him into thinking he'd seen Nick come back from the dead, something had changed about him. Now he seemed to be scared of everything, and he'd gone from being the biggest bully in the sixth grade to being the biggest tattletale. The big boy was pacing slowly back and forth as though waiting for someone.

"Do you think he knows we're here?" Carter asked.

"How could he?" Nick said. "We were careful to make sure he didn't follow us when we left our houses."

"He's sneaky," Angelo said. "Like a cat."

"A cat with huge muscles and premature facial hair," Carter said.

Nick pointed down the side of the hill to a run-down house with grass that hadn't been mowed in months. "If we sneak through Mr. Dashner's backyard, we can get to the street without Frankenstein spotting us."

Carter swallowed hard. "And if Old Man Dashner sees us, he'll call the cops. He hates kids."

"The windows are dark," Angelo whispered. "Maybe he isn't home."

Carter bit his lower lip. "Or maybe that's what he wants you to think."

Nick checked on Cody, who had stopped pacing and was looking directly at them, almost as if he could see through the dark. "I don't know about you, but I would seriously rather take my chances with Mr. Dashner than deal with the new Frankenstein."

Carter and Angelo nodded. Keeping as low as they could, they crept down the side of the hill until they were almost at the edge of Mr. Dashner's backyard. "Do you see anything?" Nick asked, peering at the dark house.

"I wish I did," Carter said. "When you *can't* see him is when he's the most dangerous."

Angelo pointed to the left side of the yard. "Let's stick close to the fence. That way, if he's home, it will be harder for him to see us."

"Or easier for him to *trap* us," Carter muttered.

One at a time, they crawled into the deep grass. The yard smelled like dog doo, although Nick was pretty sure Mr. Dashner didn't have a dog. The fence was old and saggy looking. Nick made sure not to touch any of the boards, afraid that if he did the whole thing might fall over.

"I think I saw a bear trap over there," Carter said.

"Shush." Angelo pointed to a row of tall pyracantha bushes along the side of the house. "Stick close to those," he whispered. "But don't touch them. The thorns are like needles."

Nick and Carter followed Angelo as he crawled across the grass, past the bushes, and out to the driveway. Once they were there, they got to their feet and ran to the sidewalk.

"We made it," Carter panted, stopping in the glow of a streetlight.

Nick grinned. "Dashner, zero. Frankenstein, zero. The Three Monsterteers win in a landslide."

At that moment a shadow fell across the three of them. They turned to see Cody standing less than three feet away.

"C-Cody," Carter stammered, backing away. "What are you doing?"

"Angie and her friends told me I might find you here."

"What do you want?" Nick asked, afraid to hear the answer.

9

"Do you know how much trouble you can get in for trespassing on private property?" Cody asked. "And it's way too dark to be hiking around the park. Someone could sprain an ankle or trip over a log. You would never know it, but most accidents happen within ten blocks of home."

"Yeah, we'll be more careful next time," Carter said.

"I hope so." Cody rubbed his hands together anxiously. "Because I'd hate to have to tell your parents on you. Even though it would be for your own good."

Nick sighed. He kind of wished for the good old days when all they had to worry about was getting beat up.

CHAPTER 2

I'M MORE OF A POLO FAN

"Hey, Mrs. B," Carter said the next morning as Nick's mom walked into the kitchen. It was Friday and the boys were sitting around the table before school, planning their activities for the night.

"I'm thinking we should film the cat scene," Nick said, eating a bowl of cereal. "I know a couple of neighbors that have, like, twenty in their yards."

Carter, who had just finished his third bowl of apple cinnamon Cheerios, slurped down his sugar-laden milk and burped. "Sorry, Mrs. B."

"Don't forget the mummy marathon," Angelo said.

"What's this about mummies?" Mom asked, sticking two slices of wheat bread into the toaster.

"Twelve hours of back-to-back mummy movies, commercial free," Carter said. "It's gonna be awesome sauce."

Mom got a look on her face Nick recognized immediately and he quickly jumped in. "All of our homework's done. It's not a school night, and you said Angelo and Carter could sleep over. Remember?"

"I said they could *sleep* over, not stay up all night watching that . . . *garbage*."

Angelo choked on his cereal.

Nick could see a train wreck of epic proportions coming if he didn't do something fast. "It's not garbage. It's educational. You learn about Egyptian culture, the pyramids, history, hieroglyphics . . ."

Mom shook her head and got out a jar of peach marmalade. "All while innocent people get slaughtered by mummified corpses."

"Oh, yeah." Carter rubbed his hands together. "That's the best part."

Nick shot Angelo a look of desperation. The bridge was out and the train wasn't slowing down.

"Of course we'll be working on our project for the young authors and artists contest first," Angelo said.

Mom perked up. "Really? That sounds interesting."

Could it be the wreck had just been averted? Nick

12

winked at his friends. "Yeah, we're totally into building a brighter tomorrow."

"Now that sounds like something worthwhile," Mom said. "You should do more things like that."

Disaster averted.

"I turn into a mutant rat and eat all the cats in the neighborhood," Carter said, before Nick or Angelo could stop him. He might as well have placed a bomb directly under the railroad tracks. Mom's lips pressed so tightly together they nearly disappeared.

Nick quickly grabbed the contest guidelines. "We're making a movie," he said. "About curing diseases. There are a bunch of schools competing. Even some private schools. American Leadership Academy, Walnut Creek Christian, Sumina Prep."

"Sumina?" Angelo said. "That's the school Pleasant Hill High is playing tonight."

"Playing?" Mom edged nearer to the table and Nick sensed a trap.

Angelo nodded, completely unaware. "Yeah, it's the last football game of the regular season. It's supposed to be a blowout. Pleasant Hill hasn't lost a game all season, and Sumina is a small private school that's only been around a couple of years. Some of the kids were talking about going."

13

Mom grinned evilly.

"But *we* can't!" Nick blurted. "We have to make our movie."

"I understand," Mom said, spreading the marmalade on her toast. "The arts are very important."

They were right at the bridge and the train was still in danger. Was there any way to avoid going over? Nick nodded. "Um, right."

"Just be aware that you won't be watching any mummy movies until you go to the football game and bring me back a full report. I'm going to get you out doing real activities if it kills me."

Crash and burn.

"Come on, dude, loan me a buck and a half," Carter begged Angelo, clasping his hands in front of his chest.

"You still owe me five dollars from all the frozen bananas I bought you last summer," Angelo said as he, Nick, and Carter walked along the Pleasant Hill High School bleachers looking for a place to watch the night's football game.

Nick glanced toward the field and scowled. He couldn't believe his mom was making him miss a mummy marathon to watch a stupid football game. At least Cody wasn't here.

"According to the paper the Fighting Rams might win state," Angelo said.

"Who cares?" Nick muttered. "We're talking about twelve straight hours of mummies. Are you telling me you'd rather watch a bunch of guys smashing each other to the ground than *Bubba Ho-tep*? Elvis and JFK fight a mummy."

Angelo shifted the monster notebook from his left arm to his right. "Technically, the character played by Ossie Davis only *thinks* he's JFK, dyed black and left in a nursing home by Lyndon Johnson. The viewer is left to assume Jack is delusional. Although there *is* that scar . . ."

Nick shook his head. Angelo definitely knew his monster movies. Maybe a little too well at times. But none of that mattered now because they were stuck here, watching a *real* activity.

The Pleasant Hill football players were busy stretching and going through their pre-game warm-ups under the stadium lights while the Pleasant Hill band marched around the field. His mom might call this real, but Nick called it really boring. A bunch of jocks fighting over a dumb ball. Now if they were vampires and genetically altered gorillas fighting over an anti-matter bomb, *that* would be exciting.

As the boys worked their way along the home side of the stadium, Carter turned to Nick. He ran his fingers through his short hair. After school he'd dyed it half light blue and half orange—PHHS's school colors—and it looked like someone had attacked the back of it with a pair of hedge trimmers. "What do you say, Nick? Lend me a dollar and a half. Can't you smell that meat grilling at the snack shack? I'm dying here."

"I thought hamburgers were a dollar."

"They are." Carter bounced from one foot to the other. "And I have fifty cents. So if you give me a buck fifty, I can buy two."

"You just ate dinner," Angelo said.

Carter, who was a good foot shorter than Angelo and as skinny as a post despite eating almost nonstop, rolled his eyes. "That was almost an hour ago. I'm *starving!*"

"I think you must have been bitten by a mosquito when you were a baby," Nick said. "Did you know they can eat four times their own weight in blood?"

Carter's eyes lit up. "Rob Wells says if you tense your muscles once a mosquito starts sucking, you can make it blow up."

"Whatever." Nick chuckled. Rob Wells was the biggest liar in sixth grade. He once claimed for over a month that he would be leaving soon because he'd been invited to attend wizard school.

"No. Totally serious!" Carter drew an *X* over his heart with one finger. "Rob says he did it at camp. The mosquito couldn't get loose from his arm, so it kept sucking and sucking, swelling up until it was the size of a baby sparrow. Then, bam! Blood and mosquito guts everywhere!"

Angelo clicked his tongue. "That's an urban legend. Mosquitoes draw blood from capillaries on the outer layer of the skin. They don't get anywhere near muscles."

Nick pointed to an open bench. "This looks good."

The boys were just sitting down when a bossy voice called out, "Hey, if it isn't the Three Mouseketeers." Nick turned to see Angie Hollingsworth and her friends Tiffany Staheli and Dana Lyon sitting right behind them.

CHAPTER 3

PERSONALLY, I PREFER A MORE CHALLENGING GAME, LIKE *TWO QUESTIONS*

"That's Monsterteers," Carter said. "But I can understand the mistake since the three of you are probably terrified of mice."

Angie, a short girl with flaming red hair and a take-charge expression in her bright green eyes, was one of the most annoying people Nick knew. She and her friends were in the same sixth-grade class as the boys and were constantly trying to prove they were smarter, stronger, and better. That would have been obnoxious enough, but what made the girls almost unbearable was their belief that they were even bigger monster fanatics than Nick and his friends.

"Let's move," Nick said. "I'd rather sit in the nose-bleed seats than listen to *them* all night."

"Probably a good idea," Dana said. "I'd hate to spend the whole game explaining everything to you."

That was exactly the problem. Dana was a sports nut. Tiffany was a fashion expert and a gossip. Angie was just a know-it-all in general. And they were always bragging about how smart they were.

"I'm not going anywhere." Carter scrunched up his face, as if in pain. "In fact, I'm thinking about taking off my shoes, so you girls might want to move."

"That's so gross," Tiffany said, peering over the tops of the sunglasses she was wearing despite the fact that it was night. Unlike most of the kids at the game, who were dressed in jeans and sweatshirts or sweaters, Tiffany looked like she'd just stepped out of a fashion magazine. "What's wrong with your hair? Do you have mange or something?"

Carter's face went red. "It's a ram, for the game. Maybe you should try taking off those shades so you can actually see."

The three girls burst into giggles. Nick had to admit that whatever Carter had tried to shave into the back of his head didn't look anything like a ram. And he had no idea how they were going to work it into the movie.

"I'm surprised you three are even here, with all the big news," Tiffany said.

"Nick's mom made us," Angelo said, flipping through his notebook. "We have to watch the entire game and report back before we see the mummy marathon. But I'm sure you wouldn't care about something like that."

"We're recording it," Dana said with a smug look.

Nick hadn't wanted to come to the game. And it would be that much worse if he had to spend it sitting in front of Angie. But he couldn't help asking, "What *news*?"

Angie smirked. "They haven't heard."

Carter, who had been practically drooling as he watched a man two seats over finish a huge chili-cheese dog, wiped his lips with the back of his hand. "Heard what? That your face was voted most likely to cause small children to run screaming?"

Tiffany adjusted her silk scarf. "That's very amusing. If you're a second-grader. As it happens, the police are—"

"Quiet," Angie shushed her. "They aren't interested in corpses anyway."

Angelo looked up from his pages as though Angie had just slapped him. "Did you say something about corpses?" He, Nick, and Carter looked at one another. The three of them had recently gotten some firsthand experience with the dead and undead. This couldn't have anything to do with that. Could it?

"I'm sure it wouldn't interest you," Angie said. She looked around. "Maybe I'll head down to the snack shack. I think I could use a burger right about now."

Carter moaned.

"Fine," Nick said, admitting defeat. "Tell us about the corpses."

Angie looked at her friends and the three of them grinned conspiratorially. "Why don't we play twenty questions? If you guess the right answer in twenty questions or less, we'll tell you."

"And if we don't?" Nick asked, sensing a trap.

Angie tapped her chin, appearing deep in thought. "If you don't guess the answer correctly, you have to answer one question of ours."

Angelo shook his head ever so slightly. Nick knew what he was thinking. A few weeks earlier, the boys had survived a close call with a group of zombies. They'd barely managed to get things fixed before Angie and her friends could discover the truth, but it was close. No doubt that's what Angie was planning on asking about.

"It's a deal!" Carter said before Nick could respond.

21

"But you have to throw in a burger."

"Done." Angie's eyes gleamed, and Nick knew they had been suckered. But it was too late to back out now without looking like a bunch of chickens.

Nick thought carefully before asking his first question. He needed to find out if there were zombies in town, without giving away what had happened to him and his friends before. "Have any of you seen these corpses?"

"Right, we spend all day hanging out with dead bodies." Tiffany wrinkled her nose.

"No," Dana said. "We have not seen the corpses."

Well that was good.

"Has *anyone* seen the corpses?" Carter asked, clearly anxious to win the game. "Like, have the bodies been on TV?"

Angie gave Carter a strange look before answering, "Yes. And no. Those are questions two and three."

"*Three?*" Carter sputtered. "What kind of—"

Angelo slapped a hand across Carter's mouth before he could waste another one of their questions. "Of course *someone* has seen the corpses," he whispered. "That was a waste of a question. But at least we know the corpses haven't been on TV and the girls haven't seen them."

If no one had seen the corpses that meant they probably hadn't turned into zombies. Down on the field, the players were lining up for the coin toss that would decide who would get the ball first.

Angelo leafed through his book as if hoping some kind of clue were inside. "You already said something about the news, so we know it's important. The question is, did something happen to the bodies before or after their deaths?"

"Yes or no questions only," Angie said at once.

Angelo huffed. "Fine. Did something unusual happen to the people *before* they died?"

"No." Tiffany shook back her dark hair. "Ready to admit defeat?"

"Not even close," Nick said. Angelo was on the right track. They just needed to figure out what made the bodies newsworthy. "Did something happen to them in the hospital after their deaths?"

Dana narrowed her eyes. "That's two questions."

"Two qualifiers, but only one question," Angelo corrected. "Yes or no?"

"No," Angie said. Nick started to sweat. They were already a quarter of the way through their questions and they didn't seem to be much closer than when they'd started.

"Huddle up," he said. As the Three Monsterteers put their heads together to figure out a strategy, Angie and her friends grinned with cocky self-assurance. By the time they came up with their next question, the whistle had blown and the game had started.

Nick couldn't care less about what was happening on the field. Even if he had been a football fan, Sumina Prep was a tiny school made up completely of kids born outside the country. Most of them probably hadn't even touched a football before coming to the United States. It wasn't going to be much of a game.

"Were the bodies of anyone famous?" Nick asked.

"No," Angie said. "That's six."

Over the next forty-five minutes, Nick and his friends worked slowly through the rest of their twenty questions. By the time they reached their last one, Nick knew they were in trouble. "Okay," he whispered to Carter and Angelo. "Two people recently died here in town. They aren't famous but they made the news after they died. They weren't murdered and their bodies don't appear to have come back to life. Whatever happened took place in the cemetery by my house. They weren't mutilated, sacrificed, or drained of their blood. And," he added, glaring at Carter, "they didn't climb out of their graves and dance the hokeypokey."

"*What?*" Carter said, his eyes big and round. "It could happen."

As Nick pondered what their last question should be, the crowd on their side of the field gave out a huge groan, and Nick looked down to see a player from the other team smash two Pleasant Hill players out of the way to go in for a touchdown. Nick was amazed to see it was nearly halftime and Sumina Prep was up 42 to 3. He looked down at the players on their team and rubbed his eyes. They were all huge—like the professional teams his dad watched on TV.

"Do you give up?" Tiffany asked, batting her long eyelashes. "Or are you just trying to stall until the end of the game?"

"We don't give up and we're not stalling." He looked at Angelo and nodded. This last question was their only hope.

Angelo coughed into his hand and looked down at his notes before slowly asking, "Are the bodies still in the cemetery?"

Angie's face tightened. Her eyes narrowed.

That was it! They'd nailed it with their last question.

"No," Dana said, finally. "They aren't."

Nick smiled with satisfaction. It all made sense now. The bodies weren't news because of who they were.

25

They were news because someone had taken them. *Body snatchers.* The thought sent thrills down his spine. But first he had to give his answer and win the game.

He sneered at Angie, relishing the look of defeat on her face. She knew he had it and there was nothing she could do about it.

But before he could answer, the whistle blew, signaling the end of the first half, and the band marched onto the field. People began getting out of their seats to buy snacks. Carter looked around anxiously. "Can I have my hamburger now?"

"No," Angie snapped.

Dana's face lit up. "And that's your twenty-first question. You lose."

"What?" Nick looked around. "That wasn't a question. I mean it was, but it doesn't count."

"Dana's right." Tiffany lifted her hands in the air like she was doing the wave. "No one said anything about what kind of questions count."

Nick looked to his friends, searching for a way to get out of this. Clearly Carter's question hadn't been part of the contest. But they hadn't set up any kind of rules. Angelo shrugged and scribbled in his notebook. Carter stared at his feet.

"For what it's worth," Angie said, "two bodies were

dug up from the Garden of Hope Cemetery last night. The police think it might have been some kind of prank. But they have no clues. Too bad. You were so-o-o-o close." She laced her fingers and flexed her hands. "Now it's our turn. Are you ready for your question, *Mouseketeers*?"

Angelo looked quickly up from his notes with a smile so wide he looked like a denture commercial. What was he so happy about? "*Monster*-teers," he said. "And the answer is yes. We are ready. Unfortunately for you, that was your question and *you* only get one."

CHAPTER 4

THIS IS TAKING THE FIVE-SECOND RULE WAY TOO FAR

Angie fumed, but there was no way around it. If Carter's question counted, hers did too.

"Imagine how awesome it would be to add shots of freshly robbed graves to our movie," Angelo said, closing his notebook. "If we hurry, we can get to the cemetery by ten."

"You're going now?" asked Dana. She seemed impressed.

"That, uh, might not be the best idea," Carter said. He pointed his thumb toward Nick. "Remember what happened last time we went to the cemetery?"

Nick was aching to go see the location where real

modern-day body snatchers had dug up actual corpses. He was already thinking about ways he could add them into the script. But he found himself agreeing with Carter. The last time the boys had been to the cemetery, some pretty crazy stuff had happened—including discovering that as a result of being undead for a time, Nick could actually see and talk to ghosts.

He wasn't sure whether the ability had worn off or not, but he decided he'd rather test that in the light of day. Also, he was pretty sure if they went to the cemetery now, the girls would follow. That was the last thing he wanted.

"We promised my mom we'd stay till the end of the game," he said.

"Scared of the dark?" Angie flapped her arms and made chicken noises. "Brawk, brawk, brawwwk."

"I don't see you three going," Nick said.

Tiffany held up her cell phone, which was red and white with shiny pink rhinestones. "We've already been and I've got the pictures to prove it."

"You took photographs?" Angelo rubbed his glasses on the front of his shirt. "Could I, maybe, see them?"

Angie nodded grudgingly. "Go ahead. Even if you are all a bunch of cheaters."

"We didn't cheat any more than you did," Nick said.

But he leaned over the cell phone just as eagerly as everyone else.

The first picture showed a mound of dirt surrounded by yellow police tape. "The police wouldn't let us enter their crime scene," Tiffany explained. "But this one shows the actual hole." She slid the screen to the next picture with the tip of her finger.

"Look," Angelo said, gasping with excitement. He pointed out a small pile near the edge of the grave. "They took the body but left the clothes."

Dana nodded. "Just like they did in the early 1800s. Back then, technically, a body didn't belong to anyone. As long as you left any clothing or jewelry, it was only a misdemeanor to steal a body. And doctors paid a lot of money for a corpse."

"Wow, that's right." Angelo looked amazed that someone knew as much as he did about anything— especially something like body snatching.

Nick couldn't help smiling. He'd never seen his friend speechless before. "Hang on," he said. "You're saying doctors paid money for dead bodies?" He'd heard of body snatchers, but he always figured they dug up the corpses for secret ceremonies or something.

"Lots," Dana said. "Medical students and surgeons. They needed bodies to dissect and they couldn't get enough legally. The body snatchers sold the teeth, too, to be made into dentures."

"They stuck dead people's teeth into their mouths?" Carter's face went white. For once he appeared to have heard something that grossed out even him.

Down on the field, halftime was over and the Sumina Prep players were demolishing the Rams. Nick had no idea how a tiny private school had fielded enough good players to beat a top contender for state champion. And they weren't just beating them, they were knocking them around like rag dolls. Still, Nick was far more interested in what Dana was saying.

"How do you know all this?" he asked.

"Dana's totally into creepy old stuff," Tiffany said. "She's like a fangirl for body snatchers."

"Grave robbers," Dana said.

"Resurrectionists," Angelo added, recovering his wits.

"Sack-'em-up men," Dana countered. *She was good.*

"Wait a minute," Angie said, holding out her hands. "Are you saying you think whoever took these bodies is selling them to doctors?" Nick remembered that Angie's mom worked at the hospital. He couldn't recall for sure whether she was a nurse, a doctor, or did paperwork. But whatever it was, Angie was clearly upset.

"No," Dana and Angelo both said at the same time. The two of them looked at each other for a moment.

"Doctors don't buy corpses from grave robbers anymore," Angelo said. "Stealing bodies is a crime now."

"Besides," Dana said, "there are plenty of legal ways to obtain corpses. Lots of people donate their bodies to science."

Nick was impressed. He'd always thought of Dana as a dumb jock. But listening to her talk, he had to admit she was pretty smart too.

Around the stadium, people began heading toward the exits even though there was still almost a full quarter to go in the game. Surprisingly, the visitors' side of the stadium was nearly empty. "So if it wasn't for money, you think some guy dug up the bodies for a joke?"

"Not some *guy*," Dana said. "Some *guys*. It would take at least two strong men to dig up a coffin and pull out the body."

Angelo nodded, pointing at the picture on Tiffany's phone. "See how only part of the grave is open? They dig out the top half or so. Then one guy goes down in the hole, breaks open the coffin, and loops a rope around the chest of the corpse. The other guy pulls on the rope, and presto, one dead body."

Tiffany wrinkled her nose. "That's nasty."

"It's actually quite fascinating to study," Angelo said. "The resurrectionists used wooden shovels because they were quieter than metal, and lanterns with only a small opening so villagers wouldn't catch them taking the bodies." He looked up from the phone and blinked as though realizing what he'd just said. But Dana was bobbing her head up and down.

For the next ten minutes the two of them went on and on about *mortsafes* and methods of stealing bodies Nick had never imagined. It was almost like they were speaking a different language.

Angie took the phone and flipped through the rest of the pictures. "So here's what I don't get. If people don't buy bodies anymore, why did someone go to all the trouble of stealing these?"

Nick had been wondering the exact same thing. But he wasn't about to let Angie know it. Instead he gave a big yawn as if he were bored by the whole conversation, while still listening carefully.

"Body snatching isn't near as uncommon as you might think," Dana said. "There are all kinds of reasons for taking corpses."

Angelo turned to a page in his notebook. "Abraham Lincoln's body was dug up and reburied ten times."

33

"And don't forget Alexander the Great," Dana said.

Angelo's face took on a look of concentration. "St. Nicholas."

Dana looked every bit as determined not to be outdone. "Einstein's brain."

During the last minutes of the game, Dana and Angelo continued to compare stories of missing or stolen dead people. It was like a gruesome debate—the two of them trying to prove who knew the most. As far as Nick was concerned it didn't mean much one way or the other. They'd already determined the bodies in the local cemetery weren't from anyone famous. And if they weren't stolen for money, why were they taken? The possibilities were interesting, to say the least.

When the game finally ended in a humiliating 77-to-10 loss, the whistle blew and the Pleasant Hill band launched into a listless rendition of the school song. The Rams' coach jogged slowly out to the middle of the field, slouched over as if he carried a heavy weight on his back. His team had been destroyed by a school he probably thought was going to be a piece of cake.

The Sumina coach, who also walked out to the middle of the field and shook hands, was tall, with bony arms and stilt-thin legs. He appeared to be like a hundred years old. Thick-rimmed glasses and wild gray hair made him look more like a history professor than a football coach. His long, pale face was sort of creepy.

"What are you doing?" Tiffany shrieked.

Nick spun around, his mind imagining dead bodies or worse. Instead, he found Tiffany staring horrified at Carter, who was standing several rows back, wolfing down a piece of pizza. "You want some?" he asked, holding out a greasy slice.

Tiffany put a hand over her mouth as though she were about to throw up.

"Where did you get that?" Nick asked. He was pretty sure he didn't want to know.

"It's like a buffet up here." Carter held up a pizza box with several cold pieces inside and a half empty carton of popcorn. "Who'd have thought people would leave all this food uneaten? Guess the game must have ruined their appetites." He climbed over a couple of benches. "Look, Milk Duds!"

Angie frowned. "Your friend is disgusting."

Nick couldn't really disagree.

"You know," Angelo said. "If we could actually figure out who the body snatchers are, the publicity would almost guarantee that our movie would win the contest."

"Totally," Nick said. "You, me, and Carter will

figure out who's stealing bodies while Angie and her friends . . . play house. Or whatever it is girls do."

"Fat chance," Angie snarled. "You wouldn't even know about the bodies if we hadn't told you. You'll still be tying your shoelaces when we work it all out. That is if you can ever pull your friend away from his scavenging. I think he just scraped up a piece of cheese someone stepped on."

Angelo and Dana glanced at each other while Nick steamed. What was the deal with his friends? One seemed to want to hang out with *girls* while the other wanted to search for half-eaten hot dogs. He couldn't decide which was more disgusting.

"Who's that?" Tiffany asked.

Nick followed her pointing finger to see a strange figure walking across the empty field. The man—or was it a woman?—looked like no one Nick had ever seen before. Cloaked in a long black overcoat and sunglasses, he seemed to be searching for something on the field. Every so often, he stopped to pick something up or look closely at the grass.

"Equipment manager?" Angie suggested. "Maybe he's looking for a mouthpiece."

"I've never seen a manager who looked like that," Dana said. The figure stopped, knelt on the ground, and appeared to smell the grass. Nick couldn't imagine any reason for doing that.

"He's even freakier than Carter," Angela said.

The man looked directly up at the kids, who were the only ones still up in the bleachers. He seemed to realize they were watching him and scrambled to his feet. As he raced off the field, something dropped out from under his coat to the grass. The man apparently didn't notice. He ran to the tunnel with awkward crab-like steps and disappeared into the darkness that led to the locker rooms.

"What did he drop?" Angelo asked, squinting.

Dana cupped her hands to her eyes. "It doesn't look like a piece of equipment."

Nick looked from Angelo, who was squeezing his monster notebook, to Carter, who was wiping a mustard stain from his chin. Whatever the guy had dropped, he wanted to reach it before the girls could. "Come on!" he shouted, breaking into a run.

CHAPTER 5

NOW THIS IS WHAT I CALL AN ARMS RACE

Nick raced down the bleachers, hurdling benches and jumping steps in an effort to beat the girls to the field.

"Get back here!" Angie shouted from close behind him. "We saw it first."

He had no idea what the guy had dropped. For all Nick knew it was a sweaty hip pad. But he was still stinging from Angie finding out about the missing corpses before he did, and he wasn't about to get beat by a girl.

At the bottom of the steps, a metal railing separated the bleachers from a short drop to the grass. Still running, Nick grabbed the bar and hurdled over. Before he could clear the rail completely, a hand closed around his ankle. Off balance, he fell to the ground.

A second later Angie landed on his stomach, knocking all the air out of his chest with a *woof.* "Cheater," she growled, crawling across the grass. Still trying to catch his breath, Nick wrapped both arms around her leg and held on as she tried to get to her feet.

"Not . . . yours," he gasped.

A tall shape leaped gracefully over both of them, and Nick had a moment of hope that Angelo was going to get there first before seeing Dana lope across the football field like a wide receiver racing for a pass. A moment later Angelo ran past far less gracefully, the pages of his notebook flapping as he huffed and puffed.

Nick disentangled himself from Angie just as Carter and Tiffany jogged by. Carter shoved what looked like a giant pretzel into his mouth. Tiffany held down her fluttering scarf with one hand and clutched her sunglasses with the other.

Feeling like someone had hit him in the gut with a bowling ball, Nick got to his feet and shuffled across the football field to the circle of kids. Angie didn't look much better, limping beside him.

"What is it?" Nick called hoarsely.

Angelo looked back, his face pale. "Well . . ."

"Whatever it is, it's ours," Angie said, pushing her way past the other kids.

Carter stepped backward, letting the last of his pretzel drop to the grass. "You can have it."

As the circle of kids parted, Nick caught a glimpse of what they'd all been staring at. Nestled in the bright green grass, almost exactly balanced across the fifty yard line, was what looked for all the world like a severed human forearm.

Angie's sneakers skidded as she came to a quick halt. "That's not real, is it?"

Angelo licked his lips, his glasses fogging in the cold night air as he breathed heavily. "Based on the . . ." He couldn't seem to finish his thought.

Nick couldn't believe they were falling for it. It was totally fake. "Get real. It's just a prop—like they use in the movies. Probably some player from Sumina Prep playing a trick on us." Fake-looking or not, it was cool. He could just imagine putting it in his trick-or-treat bag the next Halloween and freaking out all the health nuts who tried to give him apples.

Before anyone else could make a move, he reached down and grabbed the arm by the wrist. It felt warm. He was trying to understand how that could be, when the stadium lights went out with a loud clang.

In the sudden darkness, something banged against Nick's leg and he stumbled to the side. Someone screamed. Angie? Tiffany? Carter?

The arm seemed to twitch in his grip and fingers closed around his wrist, nails digging into his skin. With a howl, Nick flung the arm away. Someone rammed into his side and he flew through the darkness, getting a mouthful of mud and grass as he hit the turf.

Somebody grunted and another scream tore through the night.

"Let go of me," shouted a voice that he was pretty sure belonged to Angelo.

All around Nick, people were running and yelling. A foot kicked him in the head and green and red lights spun before his eyes like an out-of-control Christmas tree.

"Take that!" yelled a voice that could only be Angie, and something gave an animal-like squeal that made Nick's arms break out in goose bumps. A terrible smell filled the air and his eyes started to water.

All at once, a bright light lit up the field. Lying on the ground, Nick could see the other kids spread out around him. Angelo was standing a few feet away, clutching his monster notebook protectively to his chest. Off to his left, Dana was standing in a karate pose, legs spread, one in front of the other, one hand in front of her, the other above her head like a blade waiting to drop. Angie was on the other side of them holding a small white canister.

A tangled shape was several yards away, nearly outside of the light's range. It took Nick a moment to realize it was Carter and Tiffany, clinging desperately to each other.

"What in the name of Jiminy Cricket is going on here?" a nasal voice called. Holding a flashlight in one hand, a man in a green jumpsuit stepped toward the kids. As the man swiveled the beam toward his face, Nick could see two lines of snot running from his nose. His eyes were pools of red.

"Get back or I'll give you a faceful of pepper spray," Angie said, pointing her canister in his direction.

The man swiped his arm across his eyes, and Angelo said, "Pretty sure you already did."

Tiffany and Carter, realizing who they were holding, quickly dropped their arms and stepped away from one another—Carter with an embarrassed chuckle, Tiffany with a snort of pure disgust.

Nick's first thought was that the man with the flashlight was the same person they'd seen hurrying around the field. A second look and he realized that couldn't be. This man had short gray hair and was dressed in what looked like a gardener's outfit with the name Cebrowski stitched over the pocket. He wiped his nose with his sleeve and gave the kids a bleary-eyed glare.

"You knobbly-kneed carpet crawlers ain't supposed to be down here." He pointed his light at Angie. "Put that poison down before I call the police."

"It's not poison. It's pepper spray," Angie said. "And I'm not putting it anywhere until you tell me why you attacked us."

Despite his complete loathing for her, Nick had to admit Angie had guts, standing up to an adult that way.

Mr. Cebrowski seemed taken aback by Angie's accusation. He lowered his light and wiped his streaming eyes again. "What the flying fish are you talking about? I was only shutting down the field, just like always, when I heard screaming. I came running over to see what was wrong when somebody gave me a snootful of that firewater."

"I think he might be telling the truth," Dana said, lowering her hands. "Whoever hit me was stronger than him."

Nick nodded. He couldn't imagine the man in front

of him hitting him hard enough to send him flying the way he had.

Carter and Tiffany were uncharacteristically quiet, edging away from each other and refusing to make eye contact. But Angie wasn't backing down just yet. "I suppose you don't know anything about that arm?"

"Arm, you say?" the man asked, looking dubiously at his own two.

"A severed arm. It was on the field until Nick picked it up," Angelo said. He and the other kids looked toward Nick.

In all the excitement Nick had completely forgotten about the arm. He'd thrown it somewhere. But when he looked around, the arm was nowhere to be seen.

CHAPTER 6

I REMEMBER THE FIRST TIME I FOUGHT OVER A GIRL . . . AND HER COFFIN

Saturday morning, the boys jumped onto the internet first thing to see if there was any news from either the football game or the cemetery. Other than a sports story about the lopsided score and a short article about what the paper was calling graveyard vandalism, there was nothing new.

"The police are probably trying to downplay the body snatching so people don't freak out," Angelo said.

"You three are up early," Mom said, coming back from her morning workout with a big box of cinnamon rolls. As Mom handed out rolls and poured milk, the boys quickly closed the browser and took their food to the table.

Nick took a drink of milk and considered what had happened the night before. The more he thought about the arm, the more he realized it had to have been some kind of trick. Who would carry body parts around a football field?

Carter downed his roll in three big bites. "Are you gonna finish that?" he asked Nick.

"Yes." Nick shoved the rest of his food in his mouth before Carter could get any more ideas, and Angelo quickly did the same.

Carter grimaced. "I think I liked it better when you were a zombie."

One of the side effects of Nick's previous experience becoming a temporary member of the undead had been a loss of appetite for most foods. Now that he was back to normal, his appetite had returned.

"How was the game?" Mom asked.

"Awesome," Carter said, eyeing her roll. "Can you believe there are people who leave half-eaten food right on the bleachers where anyone can come along and take it? *Seriously*. Perfectly. Good. Pizza!"

Mom gave a stricken look to Nick, who shook his head. "Don't ask."

Dad walked into the room struggling smart phone. "Wasn't it Benjamin Franklin w pizza found is a pizza earned'?"

Mom looked from Dad to Carter and pushed plate away. "I think I just lost my appetite." Carter's eyes went wide and she shoved the cinnamon roll across the table. "Go ahead."

Carter gobbled the roll so quickly it looked like an optical illusion.

Angelo frowned at Carter. "You could say thanks."

"At least someone here has manners," Mom said.

Carter put a hand over his heart. "I'd be more formal if I didn't know you consider me a part of the family."

"He's got you there." Dad gave up on his phone and set it on the counter.

"Thanks for the food, Mrs. B," Carter said as the three boys headed for the door.

"Just promise me you won't eat anything you find on the sidewalk," Mom said.

Carter gave her a strange look. "That would be gross."

"To the cemetery?" Angelo asked, as soon as they were outside the house. "Even if we don't find any clues, we could still shoot more of the movie there. Maybe somebody steals Fitzpatrick's body after the funeral."

"Yeah," Nick said, pulling his backpack over one shoulder. "But first I have to make a stop at Cole's Deli."

Angelo raised an eyebrow.

"Talk about *me* being a pig." Carter pushed up the end of his nose.

"I'm pretty sure the food isn't for Nick," Angelo said as the three boys climbed onto their bikes. "Do you think the deli will be open this time of the morning?"

"Hope so," Nick said. "I think they serve breakfast sandwiches."

It turned out that Cole's Deli was open. But Frank, the owner, was more than a little surprised when Nick asked for a hot pastrami sandwich with extra pickles. "Kid, you're gonna have heartburn all day. Take it from Frankie."

Nick just smiled and put the sandwich in his pack along with what he'd already put there, wondering what Mr. Cole would say if he knew the real reason for the sandwich.

As they pedaled toward the cemetery, Angelo rode his bike alongside Nick's. "Are you going to say anything to your parents about the you know what?"

"Oh, yeah. I can just see me saying, 'Hey, Mom, guess what? Last night after the game I found a severed arm. Except it mysteriously disappeared after the lights went out.' I wouldn't be allowed to watch another monster movie until I wore dentures."

"Do you think the hand really moved?" Carter asked.

"Definitely not. I told you it was only a movie prop. I was just a little freaked out." Nick looked up and down the street, keeping an eye out for Cody. The last thing they needed was Cody following them to the cemetery. If he didn't want them playing on neighbors' lawns, he definitely wouldn't approve of hunting down body snatchers.

"If it was a prop, then where did it go?" Carter asked.

Nick shrugged. "Probably whoever left it there came back for it. Something that realistic-looking must have cost a ton."

At the end of the street, they stopped and waited for the light to change. "You think we can track down whoever took the corpses?" Nick asked.

"I would imagine the police have removed most of the clues," Angelo said. The light changed and the boys starting pushing their bikes across the crosswalk.

"But what if we do?" Carter said. "We'd be on the news. We'd be famous. They might even give us a parade and, like, a year's worth of hot dogs at The House of Wieners."

49

"Right. I can see it now," Nick said, his voice thick with sarcasm. "The annual Dead Body Parade. Coming soon to a graveyard near you."

"Speaking of the cemetery . . ." Angelo chewed on his lower lip. "Do you think it might be a good idea to, maybe . . . invite the girls?"

Nick stopped halfway across the street. "Are you kidding? Why would we want to bring *them*?"

Angelo ran his fingers through his hair. "You have to admit, Dana knows a lot about body snatching. I never thought she was all that smart until last night."

"Who cares?" Nick fumed. *Bring the girls. What kind of lame idea was that?* "What, do you like her or something?"

Angelo's face went white. "Take that back!" he said. The two of them tried to stare each other down.

Carter stepped between them. "Repeat after me, neither girls, nor killer shape shifters, nor horrendous body odor shall ever come between the Three Monsterteers.'"

Nick chuckled and got back on his bike. "You're the only one who needs to worry about body odor."

"Of course," Carter admitted with a wide grin. "Why do you think I threw that in? Now let's forget all this girl talk."

Unfortunately, that plan only lasted until they reached the cemetery. Angie and her friends were waiting outside the gate.

"What are you doing here?" Nick growled.

"We figured you boys would show up. Once it was *safe*. Too bad the groundskeeper has already cleaned everything up."

Darn! Angelo was right. They should have come the night before.

"And by the way, two more bodies were stolen last night," Dana said.

"Another cemetery break-in?" Angelo asked, whipping open his notebook.

"No. The hospital this time," Angie said. "I overheard my mother talking about it. Two bodies disappeared between one and three in the morning." Something about her tone made Nick suspicious. Why was she spilling the beans so easily this time?

"Too bad you won't be able to check out the scene," Tiffany said, keeping well away from Carter. "Angie's mom is going to let us into the mortuary when she works the night shift tonight. I bet we'll discover a ton of juicy clues while you play video games or root through garbage cans. Whatever it is boys do."

Nick ground his teeth. He looked at Angelo, unable

to believe what he was about to say. "Fine," he muttered. "We'll work with the three of you."

Angie burst into laughter. Not exactly the response Nick had expected. "Are you crazy?" she said. "Why would we want to work with you? We have the pictures from the cemetery—*before* it was cleaned up. We have access to the hospital morgue. And any one of us is smarter than the three of you combined."

"So you're just telling us to rub our noses in it?" Nick felt his face growing hot.

"Pretty much," Tiffany agreed. "I can't wait to post about it online."

Angelo grabbed Nick's elbow. "We need to tell them," he whispered. "Angie's right. They have no other reason to help us."

Nick's first impulse was to tell the girls to get lost. But he knew Angelo was right. There was something really weird going on here. A couple of bodies stolen from a cemetery might have been teenagers pulling a gruesome prank. But breaking into a hospital morgue was big time. Besides, he really liked the idea of adding body snatchers to their movie. And adding a mortuary scene would make it that much cooler.

"Fine," he spat, his voice so low he could barely be heard. "You take us into the hospital and I'll tell you

52

what happened to us a few weeks ago."

Angie considered his offer for a moment before shaking her head. "No dice. Whatever happened in the past is old news. We're onto something big."

Nick balled his fists. Were they trying to make him beg?

"Nick can find out what happened in the cemetery," Angelo said. "He knows some . . . *friends* who probably saw the whole thing."

"Is that true?" Angie asked. Now she was the suspicious one.

Nick nodded reluctantly. "I'm not even sure I can talk to them anymore. But if I can, Angelo's right. They probably saw what happened. They spend a lot of time around here."

"A *lot* of time," Carter said with a nervous-sounding laugh.

Angie whispered something to Dana and Tiffany. Dana whispered something back. They seemed to be disagreeing. "I don't know. What kind of people hang out in cemeteries? For all we know *they're* the grave robbers."

"Trust me," Angelo said. "They aren't the grave robbers."

Angie appeared unconvinced.

"Besides, I've got something that can help us at the mortuary. Something I made."

Dana nodded her head ever so slightly.

"Okay," Angie said. "But if you're lying, the hospital is out."

At the end of the street someone rode by on a bicycle. Nick thought the figure looked familiar. But before he could make out who it was, the bike was out of sight. He turned back to Angie.

"And if I'm not, you admit we know more about monsters than you could even dream of."

Angie sneered. "Fat chance."

CHAPTER 7

READ ON. I'M GOING TO POP OUT AND MAKE MYSELF A SANDWICH

"Bringing the girls is a bad idea," Nick whispered to his friends as they walked through the big metal gate.

Angelo tapped a pen against his knuckles. "What choice do we have?"

"We could always lead them inside, shove them into an empty grave, and run," Carter said. "Kind of a trade-off. Someone stole a couple of bodies. We put some back."

"Seems pretty mean," Nick said. "To the ghosts."

Angie stepped up beside the boys and sniffed. "What's that smell?"

Nick opened his pack and pulled out an old pair of

dress shoes he'd taken from his father's closet and the sandwich he'd bought at the deli. The pastrami was still so hot it steamed.

"Phew, that stinks," Tiffany said, waving her hand in front of her face. "I can't tell which smells worse, that sandwich, the shoes, or Carter."

Carter nodded. "Unfortunately, we'll never know for sure since your perfume is so strong it immediately kills the sense of smell of anyone who gets a whiff."

"Let's get on with this." Angie folded her arms. "Where are these so called *friends* of yours?"

"Follow me." Nick climbed off his bike and wheeled it into the cemetery. The rest of the kids followed. The last time he was here, the ghosts had shown up fairly quickly, somehow understanding that Nick was the only person who could see or hear them. They had looked more or less like regular people, except for the fact that he could see straight through them. Unlike movie ghosts, who wailed or screeched, these ghosts just wanted to talk about what they missed most from the real world—things like shoes and sandwiches.

The thing was, the only reason he could see the ghosts was because he'd been a zombie for a while. Angelo and Carter hadn't been able to see or hear anything. And as far as Nick knew, seeing the dead might be something that wore off over time. The farther he walked into the cemetery without seeing a single ghost, the more he began to worry his ability might be gone.

"Well?" Angie demanded as Nick circled the same group of headstones a second time.

"I told you it wasn't a sure thing." Nick searched the graves for any flicker of movement.

"He's lying," Tiffany said. "We can't trust them."

Something rustled in the bushes to their left and the kids spun around. Dana picked up a stick and peered into the foliage. It was probably just a squirrel or bird. Ghosts didn't move bushes.

Nick was just getting ready to admit defeat when a familiar voice said, "Is that pastrami I smell?"

A round-faced man in an old-fashioned suit drifted out of the ground almost directly beneath Nick's feet.

"Alabaster!" Nick cried, relief flooding through him.

Angie and her friends looked around, confused, as Nick pulled the hot pastrami from his bag. He held out the sandwich and the ghost leaned over to inhale the spicy aroma. The last time Nick had been here, Alabaster Wellington confided that the thing he missed most was hot pastrami. As a ghost, he couldn't eat it. But that didn't stop him from smelling it if he tried hard enough.

57

"Merciful heavens," the ghost moaned with delight. "Pastrami! It's been so long."

Nick couldn't help smiling at the spirit's obvious pleasure. "I ordered it with spicy mustard and extra pickles."

"You, my friend, are a saint," Alabaster said.

"What's he doing?" Angie asked.

Carter rubbed his hands up and down his arms as though trying to warm himself. "Nick can talk to ghosts."

"Is this supposed to be funny?" Angie's lips tightened. "Did you bring us here as some kind of joke?"

"It's not a joke," Angelo said.

Another spirit materialized. This one was tall and sad looking. He too was dressed in a suit, but his shoeless feet poked through a pair of shabby socks. "Stenson, look what I brought you." Nick pulled his father's old dress shoes from the bag. The ghost had explained how he was buried without shoes, which meant that his toes were always cold.

"Oh-h-h." The man's eyes opened wide and he almost smiled. "You remembered."

"This is priceless," Tiffany said. "You expect us to believe he's talking to a ghost with a thing for sub sandwiches and old shoes? You guys must be really desperate."

"Not one ghost. Two," Nick said, reaching inside the shoes and removing a pair of thick black socks.

Stenson choked back a sob and a long silver tear ran along a transparent cheek past his bushy mustache.

Tiffany pulled a brush through her hair. "I can't believe you thought we'd fall for this!"

"I understand how it looks," Angelo said. "And I'm not surprised by your disbelief. But despite what you think, Nick is actually communicating with the undead. It seems to be a side effect of the fact that on Halloween he turned into, well . . . a zombie."

Angie snorted. "Of course. Why didn't you say so? How could I not have realized that the three of you weren't wearing costumes at all? You actually *were* zombies. You aren't *desperate*. You're *crazy*."

"Technically, Nick was the only one who turned into a zombie," Carter said. "Which is kind of a rip-off if you ask me."

Tiffany checked her reflection in a small mirror and put her brush back in her bag. "Let's go."

Dana gave Angelo a disappointed look. "I expected more out of you."

Stenson ran his hands lovingly over the shoes, although Nick knew the spirit couldn't actually feel them. For that matter, he wasn't sure how a ghost could have cold feet when he had no actual body. "Would you mind?" the spirit asked, gesturing toward a worn headstone.

Nick set the shoes on the grass in front of the stone. Slowly, as if by magic, the shoes and socks sunk into the grass, until they disappeared completely.

"All I can say is don't ever expect . . ." Angie's words dried up, her expression going from anger to confusion as the shoes lowered into the earth. "How did you do that?" she asked.

Dana went to the spot where the shoes had disappeared and tugged at the grass. She checked Nick's bag as if she thought he'd slipped the shoes back inside and shook her head. "They're gone."

A moment later Stenson arose from his grave, his transparent feet now wearing a pair of transparent shoes.

"How do they fit?" Nick asked.

The ghost shifted his feet left and right admiringly. He brushed away a tear. "They're perfect."

"It has to be some kind of trick." Angie stared at the grass where the shoes had been. But there was no way to explain what had just happened. She turned to her friends, completely speechless for once. Dana and Tiffany seemed just as bewildered.

"No trick," Angelo said sympathetically. "I wouldn't have believed it myself. But it's all true."

Nick turned back to Alabaster Wellington, who appeared to be drooling a little. "Can you do the same thing if I put the sandwich on your grave?"

"Alas, no," the spirit said with a sniff. "I fear the damp and worms would have a rather unsettling effect on the meat—turning an aroma of pure bliss into something more like a moldering foot. But I do thank you for your kindness. I shall return to my grave a happier man, dreaming of cured meat and crunchy pickles."

"Wait!" Nick shouted as Alabaster began to fade away. Angie jumped at his voice.

"I . . ." Nick glanced over at his friends. Now that it was time to ask the questions they'd come here for, he wondered if it was going to be all for nothing. What if the ghosts hadn't seen anything? Or what if his asking offended them? "I was—I mean, *we*—were . . . wondering if you happened to see whoever broke into the cemetery the night before last?"

Alabaster scowled and Stenson made a pained face.

"Horrible, just horrible," Alabaster said. "They desecrated the graves, leaving the spirits with nowhere to call home."

61

"Three of them," Stenson added. "The pale one and two un-men."

"What did they say?" Angelo asked, his notebook ready. Carter moved back a step as if afraid of catching something from the invisible specters. The girls still looked suspicious, but even they were paying attention.

Nick held up a finger, in a *wait a minute* motion. "What do you mean, *un-men*?"

Both of the ghosts looked extremely uncomfortable. Stenson tugged at his mustache. "Living but not living. Neither here nor there."

"Well?" Angie asked.

"They say there were three of them," Nick said. "A pale guy and two men who aren't alive or dead."

"What's that supposed to mean?" Tiffany said.

"Z-zombies?" Carter stuttered.

"Vampires?" Angelo asked, scribbling frantically.

The two ghosts looked at each other and shook their heads. "I don't think they know." Creatures that even ghosts didn't recognize? The idea both thrilled and frightened him. And he didn't think he was alone. He actually thought the ghosts were scared too.

Angie stared at a spot a few feet in front of Nick, squinting as if she might be able to see the ghosts if she tried hard enough. "Where did they take the bodies?

We need to track them down."

Alabaster and Stenson both shook their heads at once with expressions it took Nick a moment to place. The spirits were not just frightened. They were terrified.

"You must *not* go after them," Alabaster said. "The pale one is dangerous in the extreme!"

"Stay as far away as possible." Stenson tugged at the ends of his mustache so hard Nick was afraid he might pull it right off. "There are things worse even than death."

CHAPTER 8

I'LL NEVER SMELL THE SAME WAY AGAIN

That night after dinner the five of them followed Angie to the back of the hospital. "Shouldn't we go around the front?" Carter asked, glancing at the gray metal doors dimly illuminated by a buzzing fluorescent light.

"Live bodies go through the front entrance," Angie said. "Dead bodies enter here."

Nick imagined zippered bags being rolled up the ramp in front of him, and his tongue stuck to the roof of his mouth. "What exactly does your mother do?" he asked.

"She's a pathologist," Angie said. "She performs autopsies."

Angie's mom cut open dead bodies for a living. That explained a lot.

Carter pulled a Tootsie Pop from his jacket pocket and stuck it in his mouth. "Maybe we should just let the police handle this, huh, Nick?" he muttered around the candy. "You said those ghosts were pretty specific about staying away from whatever's going on here."

"Go ahead," Angie said. "Then we'll know for sure that you're all a bunch of cowards."

Nick wasn't sure. The ghosts had freaked him out. And the idea of poking around a mortuary at night was more than a little frightening. On the other hand, what kind of monster hunters would they be if they backed out at the first sign of danger?

"It's not like whoever took the bodies is still around," Dana said.

Angelo took a small metal box out of his backpack, attached a handle, and began fiddling with a pair of dials.

"Metal detector?" Nick asked.

"Something a little more helpful," Angelo said.

Dana raised an eyebrow.

"Make up your minds already. It's cold out here." Tiffany rubbed her hands together.

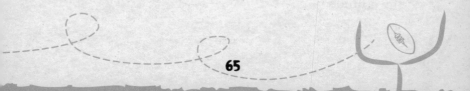

"Not as cold as the bodies in there," Angie said ominously. When it was clear none of them were backing out, she led the way through the double doors and down a green-tiled hallway. Angie pointed to a window covered from the inside by a curtain. "That's where they let people look in to identify the bodies."

Past the window was a door with a round metal grate and a card reader beside it. Angie pushed the button and spoke into the grate. "Hey, Mom, it's us."

Angelo reached into his bag and handed Nick the video camera. "Get as many shots as you can. You never can tell when we might need to splice in a good morgue shot. Especially if there's anything gruesome."

"Who said you get to take pictures?" Angie asked.

"It's for the Building a Brighter Tomorrow contest," Nick said.

Angie gave him a suspicious glare.

Nick wasn't sure what he'd expected Angie's mom to look like. Tall, with glittering eyes, a bloody apron, and a scalpel maybe. So he was surprised when the woman who opened the door was short with red hair and a warm smile. She wore a dark blue pantsuit and stylish glasses attached to a beaded chain. Mostly she looked like an older version of Angie, except without the attitude.

"Well, this is a surprise," she said. "What are you kids doing here?"

"Don't you remember?" Angie said. "You told me you'd give us a tour for our career report?"

Dr. Hollingsworth ran her fingers distractedly through her hair, taking in the group. "When you said you had a homework assignment, I thought you were bringing Tiffany and Dana."

Angie shot Nick a warning look. "Nick is very interested in a medical career. But if it's any trouble they can come back another time."

Nick got the message. Angie hadn't told her mother the real reason they were at the hospital. He'd better keep his mouth shut about the fact that this wasn't exactly a school project or risk getting booted out.

"We're also filming for a school project," Nick said, holding up the video camera. "Kids need to know how important doctors are to our future."

Carter jumped into the role enthusiastically. "Doctors are the bomb. So do you really cut people open? Is it cool or totally gross?" He pointed to a row of square metal lockers set into the wall. "Is that where you put the bodies? What do you do with the guts?"

Dr. Hollingsworth chuckled uncomfortably as though not quite sure how to respond. Carter tended to have that effect on adults.

"I'm sure as a pathologist you do a lot more than autopsies," Dana said.

Angie's mom relaxed visibly. "As a matter of fact I do. If you want to follow me, I'll show you the laboratory where I examine biopsies and test tissue samples."

What do you do with the guts? Tiffany mouthed silently as the kids followed Dr. Hollingsworth. Carter held out his hands palms up.

Angelo, who was fiddling with the dials on his box again, whispered to Nick, "Keep her occupied with the camera. I want to check something," before disappearing back into the morgue.

For the next thirty minutes, the doctor pointed out microscopes, test tubes, and a bunch of equipment Nick was sure his science teacher would go gaga over. Nick had hoped for something a little more shocking to put in their movie. He suspected she was purposefully avoiding certain parts of her job. Halfway through the tour Angelo slipped back in with the group.

"Did you find anything?" Dana whispered.

"Maybe," Angelo whispered back, mysteriously. "I won't know for sure until we get outside."

"That was really interesting, Mom," Angie said, when they finished the tour. She waved her hand behind her back in a *come-on* gesture, and the other kids quickly joined in.

"Yeah."

"It was great. Kids will be so inspired."

"Thanks for the tour. I bet we'll get an A."

"I was especially fascinated by the cytometer," Angelo said. Personally Nick thought that was a little over the top. But Dr. Hollingsworth seemed pleased, and knowing Angelo, it might be true.

Angie ran a hand across her mother's desk, and shifted around a stack of paper clips. "So, is it, um, true that a pair of bodies really disappeared last night?"

The doctor's eyes immediately went from kind to suspicious. Nick quickly turned off the camera. "Where did you hear that?" Dr. Hollingsworth demanded.

Angie shrugged. "Oh, just around."

The skin across the doctor's forehead tightened. "Well, I don't know who's saying what. There *may* have been a slipup in paperwork by an assistant who is no longer employed here. But I can tell you for a fact that no bodies *disappear* from this morgue."

"Is it possible someone snuck in?" Nick asked.

Angie's mother pointed to the entry door. "Did you see the card reader out there?"

Nick nodded.

69

"No one comes in or out without scanning their I.D. I've been chief pathologist here for nearly ten years. And not once during that time has a body gone missing under my watch." It was clear the tour had taken a direction she wasn't happy with.

"Well, thanks for the information," Nick said. "This will make an awesome report."

"If I ever die, I hope you're the one who cuts me open," Carter said.

Dr. Hollingsworth noticed Angelo's notebook. "I can assume you won't be putting anything about missing bodies in your report?"

"Absolutely not." Angelo tucked his notebook quickly away in his pack. "I'm going to write about what an amazing service pathologists provide to the community and how honored I would be to follow in your footsteps."

The doctor bit her lower lip. "Yes, well, it's time for all of you to be getting home. You've got reports to write."

"Sure." Angie gave her mom a hug and a kiss on the cheek. "I'll see you in the morning, Mom."

As the kids filed out into the hallway, Nick inspected the door more closely. The lock looked solid and he couldn't think of any way someone could trick the card reader. "Maybe it really was just a paperwork mistake," he said when they were back outside. "It might not have anything to do with the cemetery at all."

"My mom wouldn't lie," Angie said, daring anyone to disagree with her.

"I'm sure she believes it was a clerical error," Angelo said. "But someone took one or more bodies through this door recently. And from what I can tell the corpses were at least a couple of days old."

Nick stared at his friend. He knew Angelo was smart, but this was too much.

"There's no possible way you could know that," Dana said.

"*I* couldn't. But *this* can." Angelo held up the metal box. Looking at it more closely, Nick could see a dial going from one to one hundred. Two knobs beside it were labeled BASE and SENSITIVITY. At the top of the box was a red light, and underneath it was a kind of funnel-looking thing with a tiny fan inside.

"Let me guess," Carter said. "It's a Super Deluxe Automatic Body Finder. As seen on TV."

"You are so lame," Tiffany said.

"Actually he's not as far off as you might think." Angelo adjusted the sensitivity dial until the red light began to flash slowly. From somewhere inside the box

71

came a soft, *beep, beep, beep*. "This is sort of an electrical bloodhound. It uses A.S.T. to track different smells."

"A.S.T.," Dana said, her eyes lighting up. "I thought it looked familiar."

Angie didn't seem impressed. "Does someone here want to tell me what ast is?"

"Not ast, A.S.T." Dana put a hand gently onto the device as though it were the Holy Grail. "Aroma sensing technology. It's a high-tech, extremely sensitive tool for comparing one smell to another. Perfume companies use it to develop their scents. And car companies use it to make sure their cars have the right 'new car' smell. But these things cost like a hundred thousand dollars."

"Retail," Angelo agreed. "Maybe even a little more. I built it for about sixty bucks using stuff from Radio Shack, parts from a broken laptop, and some old biology equipment my mom's college was getting rid of."

Nick shook his head. "Buddy, I'm not gonna lie. You are a freaking genius. But what does any of this have to do with finding a body?"

"Let me guess," Dana said. "You calibrated your device to sniff out the aroma signature of a decaying corpse. Pure genius!"

Angelo blushed.

"Wait, wait, wait," Nick said, his head spinning. "You're saying this box of yours can tell us where the stolen bodies are?"

"It's not that easy." Angelo adjusted the sensitivity and the beeping got a little louder. "I can't tell you what body I'm following. Or who took it. But I can tell you, based on the aroma signature, approximately how long the body was dead. I adjusted my settings based on a corpse from one of the lockers inside the mortuary. If we're lucky, we might be able to follow where the body was taken from here. Like a dog tracking a scent."

Angelo began swinging the box left and right. Depending on where he moved the box, the dial went up or down and the red light flashed quicker or slower. "It looks like they took the bodies down the ramp," he said. "And across the parking lot."

Slowly, the six of them crossed the asphalt away from the light of the building.

"You think maybe we should come back in the morning?" Carter asked. "You know, when we can see better, in case some crazed maniac decides he'd rather have live bodies than dead ones?"

But Angelo wasn't listening. "I think I've got something." He jogged to the edge of the parking lot, his sensor beeping more and more quickly. "Right here," he said, stopping at the edge of a field of high, dead grass.

Nick leaned forward and pushed back the grass. There, just where Angelo had led them, was a pile of bones with bits of flesh still clinging to them.

CHAPTER 9

THIS CHAPTER REALLY TICKLES MY FUNNY BONE

Tiffany screamed and backed away from the grisly scene.

"*Now* can we call the police?" Carter begged, looking like he was going to throw up.

Angie stared at the pile of bones, ash-faced, and Nick's stomach rolled over with a sick thudding that felt like he'd gone on the carnival Tilt-A-Whirl ride one too many times. "Carter's right," he said softly. "This is something we need to turn over to adults. Preferably adults with badges and guns."

Angelo cradled his sensor, his dark eyes huge. Surprisingly, Dana seemed hardly affected at all. She knelt at the edge of the grass, examined the bones, and actually picked one of them up.

"What are you doing?" Nick yelled. "This is a crime scene."

Dana turned the bone over, smearing her fingers a dark red and Nick knew he was going to hurl. Dana returned the bone to the pile, and picked up a ball of wadded paper smeared with the same dark red. Nick had seen enough TV crime shows to know they were going to be in huge trouble for interfering with clues.

Dana unfolded the paper, looked at what was on it, and nodded. "The police might be interested all right. But only if they're really hungry."

"What are you *talking* about?" Nick asked.

"My nose might not be quite as sensitive as Angelo's box, but . . ." She sniffed a red stain on the paper, and Carter slapped a hand to his mouth, gagging. "If I'm not mistaken it's sweet and tangy."

Nick was sure she'd gone totally off her rocker until she showed them the paper and he read the words printed on it. "Big Al's Southern Bar-B-Q."

For a moment no one said a word. Then Tiffany began to giggle. Carter made a sound that was half laughter, half moan.

Ribs. Barbecued ribs. Nick couldn't believe it. But

now that he wasn't scared out of his mind, he saw what Dana had seen all along. The bones were far too small to be human. What he'd taken for torn flesh was bits of pork and what his mind convinced him was blood was only sauce.

"Barbecue." Angie guffawed. "Your high-tech gizmo led us to somebody's leftover lunch. Maybe if you re-adjust the settings it can find Carter another pizza."

Angelo stared at his device, dumbfounded.

Nick knew he shouldn't, but he couldn't help laughing. First a little chuckle. Then louder. Finally, he was laughing so hard, tears rolled from his eyes. All around him everyone except Angelo was doing the exact same thing—fear turning to relief. Carter fell on the ground, pounding the asphalt with his hands and howling, "Call the cops. Somebody stole a perfectly good meal!"

"I don't understand how this could have happened," Angelo said.

That just made the other kids laugh all the harder.

"Stop it," Dana cried, waving the food wrapper like a white flag. "I'm gonna puke."

"Right in the middle of Angelo's crime scene," Angie gasped.

Angelo tapped the dial on his box and twisted the knobs. "It doesn't make sense. I'm sure I calibrated it for the scent of human decay."

Nick wiped his eyes. He looked toward Dana, who was laughing so hard she'd started to hiccup, still waving the white wrapper. Something about the wrapper caught his attention. "Can I see that for a minute?"

"Sure." Dana giggled. "Just tell me—*hic*—you're not going to—*hic*—lick off the sauce."

Nick grinned. He turned the wrapper over and his laughter slowly faded to confusion. There was something written on the back. It wasn't exactly words. More like shapes. Triangles, circles, and *X*'s, with strange squiggles connecting them.

Angelo looked over his shoulder. "Hieroglyphics?"

Angie joined them, her laughter drying up too. "It looks like some kind of code."

The rest of the group circled around Nick to examine the strange shapes. Dana took one look and shook her head. "It's not a code. And it's not hieroglyphics."

"How can you be sure?" Tiffany asked. She tilted her head as though the writing might make more sense sideways.

Dana took the paper and flattened it out. "My dad was a coach for ten years. This looks just like what he used to write on his whiteboard. It's not a code. It's football plays. Look." She traced the lines with her finger. "This is the offensive line. The arrows show where they're supposed to block. This line shows the quarterback is going to roll out to his left and toss the ball to the halfback. Each of these patterns is a different play."

"So what?" Carter said. "Some sports nut had dinner here and littered. What does it matter?"

"It probably doesn't," Nick said. But something one of the ghosts had told him was nagging at the back of his mind. "What if Angelo's sensor *didn't* malfunction?"

"Of course it malfunctioned," Tiffany said. "It led us to a pile of pork ribs."

"Which would make sense," Angelo said, "if whoever stole the bodies also ate the ribs."

"It's too much of a coincidence." Dana crumpled up the wrapper. "You're saying some guy stole a couple of bodies, then waited around in the hospital parking lot eating a snack?"

Angie snapped her fingers. "Or he sat around in the parking lot eating while he waited for his chance to steal the bodies. Eating and drawing football plays."

Nick remembered what it was that had been bothering him. "Stenson called one of the men who stole the bodies from the cemetery *the pale one*."

Angie's mouth dropped open, then snapped shut.

"The coach," she said. "From the football game. I remember looking at Sumina Prep's coach at the end of the game and thinking how old he looked. Old and weird, with a white beard and—"

"Pale skin," Nick finished.

"I don't know." Tiffany shook her head. "Based on Angelo's device and some football plays on a wrapper, you think a football coach is stealing bodies? Seems like a stretch to me."

"Maybe not as big of a stretch as you think," Nick said. "Think about it. The team comes into town right after a pair of bodies is stolen from the cemetery. After the game we find a severed arm on the field. Late that night, somebody buys ribs from an all-night barbecue place, sketches out some football plays, and steals a pair of bodies from the hospital."

"As much as I hate to say it, I have to agree with Tiffany," Carter said. "Why would some private-school coach steal bodies?"

"The Skull and Bones Society," Angelo said.

"Huh?" Nick looked around, wondering what he'd missed. Everyone else looked confused too, except for Dana, who was nodding her head.

"The Skull and Bones Society," Angelo repeated. "It's an ultra-secret group at Princeton University. All

80

kinds of high-powered people belong to it. Even some U.S. presidents. Part of the initiation is that you have to steal something to become a member. Rumor has it that some of the members stole actual body parts—skulls and stuff of some pretty famous people."

Nick wasn't sure he was following. "So you think Sumina's football coach was a student at Princeton?"

"Maybe not," Dana said. "But maybe Sumina has their own secret society. And maybe stealing bodies is part of their initiation. Maybe the football team is part of the society." She opened the wrapper. "Some of these look pretty familiar. I can't swear it, but they look like plays Sumina was running against Pleasant Hill last night."

Carter pulled another Tootsie Pop out of his pocket. "Or maybe they use the bodies for some kind of ritual to give them power over their enemies. That could explain how they won the game."

"It's an interesting theory," Nick said. "But how can we prove it? It's not like we have any real evidence."

Angie grinned, her eyes gleaming in the moonlight. "Then we'll have to find some. The place to get it is Sumina Prep. And tomorrow night is the perfect time to go."

CHAPTER 10

TRAINS ARE A GREAT PLACE TO MEET PEOPLE

Diablo Valley, where Sumina Preparatory Academy was located, was just over twenty miles from Pleasant Hill. Not a terribly long bike ride. But all the kids agreed they'd rather go by train. The nearest BART, or Bay Area Rapid Transit, station was only a few blocks from their school, and the train would drop them off just over a mile from their destination.

Since they would be going at night, it meant not having to ride more than twenty miles each way in the dark. "Besides," Angelo pointed out, "if one of our bikes breaks down that far from home, we might end up having to call for a ride." Not a good idea, since their parents had no idea what they were up to.

The train rumbled along its elevated tracks, shaking and groaning. The kids had an entire car to themselves except for a man in a scruffy gray overcoat who'd entered, dropped into the far back seat, and started snoring immediately. Carter listened to his MP3 player, drumming on his knees to the music and sucking on the straw of a Gargantuan Gulp. Tiffany was busy checking her latest friend updates on her phone. Angelo and Dana were debating the merits of different vampire movies.

Nick was staring out the window, wondering if sneaking into the school was really such a good idea, when Angie dropped into the seat across from him. "Thinking about chickening out?" she asked.

"Not likely," he shot back. "But if we get arrested for breaking in, I'll make sure and remind the police it was your idea."

"Who said anything about breaking in? I just want to check things out. Maybe peek in a few windows."

Nick didn't believe that for a minute. They weren't going all this way to walk around and look through the blinds.

Angie twisted a strand of her red hair and Nick wondered what she was going to harass him about now. Instead, she asked, "Did you really turn into a zombie?

Or was that just a trick to make us take you into the hospital?"

Nick considered lying to her, but he decided it wasn't such a good idea, since they were all going to be working together tonight. "Yep, I was a zombie. I thought you had it figured out that night you came with your aunt and uncle to dinner."

"I nearly did. Between your stunt at the pool, your visit to the cemetery, and you smelling like the city dump. I was so close. Then I decided you'd just quit showering." Angie sighed. "What was it like?"

Nick shrugged. After years of viewing Angie as the enemy, it felt weird to tell her anything. Like giving away state secrets. "Cool at first. I didn't have to sleep. I could hold my breath almost forever. And the trick we played on Frankenstein . . ."

"Is *that* what you did?" Angie laughed. "I knew you guys had something to do with his sudden turnaround." In the back of the train, the sleeping man snorted and rolled to his other side.

"It wasn't all great, though," Nick said. "My joints started getting all wobbly, I ate this disgusting brain substitute, and I nearly got caught when my little finger fell off at dinner."

Angie clapped her hands. "That's why you threw

84

the mashed potatoes on my aunt and uncle!"

Now it was Nick's turn to laugh. "What else could I do? You would have busted me for sure if you'd spotted my pinky sticking up out of the bowl."

"I wish I could turn into a zombie." Angie frowned.

Nick almost felt sorry for her. "Trust me. You wouldn't if you knew what it took to get turned back."

Dana and Angelo crossed the train car to join them. Nick couldn't help grinning at his friend's outfit. Unlike the rest of them, who were all dressed in normal clothes, Angelo was wearing a long black leather overcoat, black gloves, and a high-tech watch that displayed the time in three different zones and a stopwatch at once.

"Love the getup." Nick snickered. "Did you bring your secret decoder ring too?"

"I'm just trying to be prepared," Angelo mumbled.

"I think it's awesome," Dana said. "I wish I'd brought gloves."

Angelo's eyes glowed at the compliment. "So, what's the plan?" he asked, opening his notebook. "Did you look up the school blueprints?"

Nick glanced at Angie, hoping she'd thought of that. "Umm . . ."

"Tell me you at least used Google Earth to get the layout," Dana said.

Angie studied the back of the seat in front of her. "It's not like we had a lot of time to prepare," she said. It was a pretty lame excuse, Nick thought. But then, he hadn't done any better.

"I guess we'll just play it by ear," he said.

Carter pulled out his earphones and joined the group. "I'm ready," he said, balancing his massive soda and MP3 player in one hand while he reached into his pocket and pulled out a paper clip, a pair of tweezers, a rock, and a rusty pocketknife.

"Ready to what?" Angie asked skeptically. "Remove a sliver or give yourself tetanus?"

"Amateurs," Carter huffed. "This happens to be my world-class lock-picking kit. I slide the knife between the door and the jamb, put the paper clip into the lock, and jiggle it with the tweezers."

"What's the rock for?" Dana asked.

Carter grinned. "If everything else fails, I throw it through the window."

"We're not breaking any windows. And we're not picking any locks. That's breaking and entering. You can get arrested for it," Nick said.

The train rocked as it rounded a turn and Angelo frowned. "What's the point of going then?"

"To see if we can find anything weird," Angie said.

"If people there really are stealing bodies, it can't exactly be an ordinary school."

"I'll tell you one thing strange about it," Tiffany said, tapping on her phone screen.

"Let me guess, their clothes are out of style," Carter sneered.

Tiffany gave him a look that could freeze lava. "That would be you, Mr. I-wear-the-same-chocolate-milk-stained-shirt-for-a-week. But you're not that far off. While the rest of you have been talking—or drumming completely out of rhythm—I did an internet search for kids who attend Sumina Prep. Believe it or not, not one student has a Facebook account, Twitter profile, or blog that I could find. In fact I couldn't find a single internet presence for any of them."

Nick rubbed his chin. Almost every kid he knew had at least one online profile and many had several. "What does that mean?"

"It means," Tiffany said, "that either the students there are really, really, strange. Or that someone is intentionally keeping them from communicating with other kids."

• • •

Twenty minutes later, the train squealed to a halt outside the Diablo Valley train station. A slow drizzle of rain fell from the dark sky and Nick zipped up his wind-breaker. He couldn't help envying Angelo's long leather coat that he'd mocked earlier.

Carter looked around the empty platform and shivered. "Does anyone else think it's more than a co-incidence that the school is located in a city called the devil's valley?"

"The city was here long before the school," Dana said.

"Right. But why did they pick this city for the school? Maybe because they perform satanic rituals? Maybe because they use dead bodies as bait for power-ful demons from another dimension?"

"Maybe your brain's been liquefied by all that soda," Tiffany said.

"At least I have a brain," Carter said. "If you pointed a light into one of your ears it would shine out the other."

Nick shoved his hands in his pockets and started down the stairs to the parking lot, trying not to think about what Alabaster and Stenson had said. Anything that could scare a ghost had to be pretty darn terrify-ing.

According to their directions, the school was just over a mile to the west, but they'd only walked a few blocks from the station when Dana pointed and said,

"Is that what I think it is?"

Nick looked where she was pointing and involuntarily stepped backward. Standing high on the edge of a bluff overlooking the rest of the town was what looked like a mansion or an old European castle pulled straight out of a horror movie. Dark turrets stabbed up at the night sky and big black windows stared down on the town like empty eye sockets.

Carter gulped. "That can't be a school. It's way too creepy."

Angelo bit his lip and checked the map. "That's got to be it."

Even Angie looked like she was having second thoughts when a hand dropped onto Nick's shoulder. He turned to find the man from the train standing right behind him.

"Gotcha," he said in an eerily familiar voice.

"Wha—what do you want?" Nick stammered, trying to pull away.

"I want to know what you guys are up to." The man took off the hat he'd worn low over his eyes and Nick recognized the face glaring at him.

It was Cody Gills.

CHAPTER 11

THERE'S A REASON I NEVER WENT TO SCHOOL ON SUNDAY

Angie jabbed a finger into Frankenstein's chest. "You followed us."

"I sure did," Cody said. "First you guys are sneaking around the cemetery. And now this. What's next? Robbing banks?"

"That was you creeping around in the bushes?" Nick asked.

"Someone has to keep an eye on you guys." He looked up at the castle-like school building. "Are you going to that house?"

"It's not a house." Angelo was the only one of them tall enough to look Cody in the eyes. "It's Sumina Prep."

"The school the Rams played Friday?" Cody's eyes widened. "You guys aren't going to vandalize it, are you? That's against the law."

"Of course not," Dana said. "We're just looking."

"And making a movie," Angelo said. "For the Building a Brighter Tomorrow contest."

Cody folded his massive arms across his chest. "If you're just making a movie, why sneak around on a Sunday night?"

Nick groaned. "This is none of your business. Just go back home, okay? I promise we won't break any laws."

Cody shook his head. "Not unless you come back too. Do you realize how much trouble you'll be in if you get caught trespassing in a private school at night?"

"We aren't going to get caught." Angie slugged Cody on the shoulder, but the big boy didn't flinch. "Look, we think the guy who runs that school is . . . well, let's just say he's doing some bad stuff. Don't you think it's our duty to find out?"

"Nope." Cody looked stubbornly from face to face. He shook his head, water splashing from his hair like a wet dog. "If you really think someone's breaking the law, call the police."

Back in the days when Cody was a bully, they might

have been able to fight him off. After all, he was big, but there were six of them. The thing was, you couldn't exactly fight someone who thought he was looking out for you.

"Fine," Nick said at last. "If you're so worried about it, come with us."

Angie looked at Nick like she couldn't believe what she was hearing.

"Huh?" Cody seemed just as surprised. His forehead wrinkled as though he were trying to figure out a tough math problem. "Is this some kind of trick?"

"No trick," Nick said. "If you're so worried about us, come with us. That way you can make sure we don't break any laws."

Cody cracked his knuckles thoughtfully. "I *guess* I could do that."

"Okay," Nick said. "Let's go."

"That might not be the best idea," Angelo whispered, as the kids turned and started up the steep winding road that led to the school.

"It's not like we had much choice," Nick whispered back. "Bringing him with us is a pain. But if we try and make him leave, he could tell someone what we're doing."

Of course they could always go home and come

another day, when Cody wasn't watching them. But if they waited, any evidence of body snatching might disappear.

Nick ducked his head, trying to keep the stinging rain out of his eyes. The air smelled like mud and wet leaves, and the wind made a sort of moaning sound as it slapped and bit at the bare trees around them. The kids grouped closer together, trying to stay warm.

"So, what are we looking for?" Cody asked, his voice booming.

"Quiet," Dana said, wiping her hair out of her eyes, "someone might hear you."

Angelo took off his glasses and scrubbed them across his shirt front. A futile gesture, since they were covered with water again seconds after he put them back on. "I told you, we're making a movie."

"That's a *good* thing," Tiffany said, tucking her hair under a paisley scarf. Even in the middle of a storm, she looked like she was on her way to a party instead of a exploring a freaky school.

"What kind of movie?" Cody asked, clearly suspicious.

"It's kind of a horror movie," Nick said. "But with an important message about the future."

By the time they reached the top of the hill, all of the

93

kids were panting from the steep climb. The only one who didn't seem winded at all was Cody, who should have been the most out of breath, considering his size.

"Aren't you tired?" Carter asked.

"Nope." Cody shrugged his broad shoulders. *He might be a pain,* Nick thought. *But you have to admit he is tough.*

From the top of the bluff, Sumina Prep looked even more intimidating. It was hard to believe anyone went to school there. Thick stone walls rose four and even five stories in places. There were no lights in the windows.

"Where are the signs?" Carter asked.

Dana tilted her head questioningly.

"You know," Carter said, pointing to the front of the building. "Buses only. No parking. PTA meeting Wednesday at nine. There aren't any signs."

"No satellite dishes either," Angelo said. "And no bike racks."

They were right. This didn't look like any school Nick had ever seen. The only sign that they hadn't been transported back into the 1700s was the thick strands of electrical cables weighing down a line of telephone poles.

"They definitely exercise, though." Dana walked to

94

the tall iron fence surrounding the back and sides of the school. On the other side of the fence were a football field, two tracks, tackling dummies, rows of tires, and lots of weights.

Tiffany took off her sunglasses and peered between the bars. "Is that a cemetery?"

Nick was sure she must be wrong. There couldn't possibly be a cemetery at a school. That would just be too freaky. And yet, staring through the driving rain, he thought he could just make out a row of headstones on the other side of a leaning picket fence far across the field.

"Maybe we better go," Cody said, cupping his hands above his head. "It's raining pretty hard. That can't be good for your camera."

"I'm not sure we have much choice," Dana said. "Peeking through windows is out." She was right. Every window on the first floor was covered with heavy wooden shutters. The only visible glass was high overhead. There was no way to reach the school grounds themselves, either, unless they wanted to scale a twenty-foot spiked fence.

Drenched and discouraged, Nick walked to the front of the school. Like the rest of the building, the entrance looked like something from a castle. Heavy wooden

95

doors banded with thick black metal made it clear visitors were unwanted. There weren't even knobs, just heavy iron rings that looked hundreds of years old.

"I'm surprised there isn't a moat," Angie said.

"Look." Angelo pointed to a series of thin rectangular openings in the stone wall. "Arrow slits. They were used by archers to hold off an enemy invasion."

Nick shook his head. "What kind of a school prepares for an invasion?" He would have sworn they were at the wrong place if not for the small brass plaque that read SUMINA PREPARATORY ACADEMY OF HIGHER LEARNING.

The one thing about the doors that didn't look ancient was the locks. Unlike the rest of the building, they appeared to be extremely modern, and extremely expensive. "I don't think your tools are going to help us, Carter." Nick grabbed one of the rings. At that moment a blue flash lit the sky, accompanied by an immediate crash of thunder.

Shocked by the closeness of the lightning strike, Nick yanked at the ring and the big door swung open.

CHAPTER 12

AS IT TURNS OUT, ANGIE AND ANGELO ARE NOT THE ONLY BRAINS

The seven kids stood at the open door, peering into the dark hallway beyond. Overhead, the clouds had gone into overdrive, dumping icy sheets of rain in an ever-increasing roar as lightning flashed all around. But no one made a move into the school.

Angie scrubbed her hands together as though trying to wash something off. "This doesn't feel right."

That might have been the biggest understatement Nick had ever heard. It was like the mouth of some ancient beast had just opened in front of them. The light on the other side of the door had an odd flickering blue tint to it, and the warm air flowing out of the building smelled old and somehow used up.

Angelo scuffed a sneaker along the edge of the entryway, hands shoved deep in his coat pockets. "The way that door just swung open, it's like someone is . . . expecting us."

They might have turned back then and there if Carter hadn't shoved his way past them and hurried into the school without a backward glance. Nick couldn't believe it.

"You said you were making a movie," Cody said. "Not breaking in."

"We didn't *break* in," Angie said, entering the school with Dana and Tiffany right behind her.

Nick turned to Angelo. "Do you think they always leave the front door unlocked?"

Angelo's monster notebook was tucked into his backpack, safe out of the rain, and Nick thought he looked naked without it. "With the rest of the school surrounded by spiked fences, protected by stone walls, and hidden behind closed shutters?" Angelo released a long, shaky breath, shook his head, and stepped through the door.

Only Nick and Cody were left standing outside in the rain. Nick brushed his dripping hair out of his eyes and looked up at the tall building. He knew the wall was straight up and down, but it seemed to be leaning over him.

Cody bit the back of his thumb. "I have a really bad feeling about this."

For once Nick agreed with him. Angelo was right—with the heavy security around the rest of the school, leaving the front doors unlocked made no sense. Either someone wanted them to come in, or else they didn't think anyone would be foolish enough to try. Neither of the options sounded particularly promising.

With the rest of his friends already inside the school, though, Nick didn't really have a choice.

"I'm going in," he said. "You can do what you want." He hoped he wasn't making a terrible mistake. If something happened to them, no one knew where they were. Cody waited a second, then hurried through the door.

Nick's first impression was that the hallway was completely lightless. Blinking, he could barely make out the other kids standing around him. As his eyes adjusted, he noticed a row of small, fluttering flames along each of the stone walls.

"What kind of school uses gas lamps?" Dana whispered. "Isn't that some sort of code violation?"

"I don't have the impression they get a lot safety inspections," Angelo said, his voice hushed.

99

Something banged right behind Nick, and he nearly peed his pants before realizing it was only the door blowing shut from the wind.

"What do we do now?" Tiffany asked. All of them were speaking softly as though they were in a library or a museum.

Angie pointed to a series of doors set into the stone walls. "I guess we could try one of those."

"Let's take out our lights," Angelo said.

Everyone except Frankenstein reached into their backpacks and pulled out a flashlight. "Why don't I get one?" he asked.

Dana turned on her light and shined it into his eyes. "Next time you follow us, come a little more prepared."

Nick turned to Carter and whispered, "I can't believe you walked right into the school like that. You are seriously one brave dude."

Clutching his light in one hand, Carter hopped from one foot to the other as if he were in pain. "It's not exactly what you think."

"Are you okay?" Nick asked.

"I gotta go, man," Carter squeaked, his face pinched.

"We just got here," Angie said.

"Not that kind of go." Carter pressed his hands to the front of his pants, bit his lips, and blurted, "I gotta

100

go whiz." Without another word he raced down the hall, his footsteps echoing as he ran in search of a bathroom. In a couple of seconds he was out of sight.

"That's what he gets for drinking his weight in soda," Tiffany said.

"Shouldn't one of us should go with him?" Cody asked.

Nick wasn't surprised when no one volunteered. The idea of leaving the group and exploring this freaky building alone was more than a little frightening. Who knew what might be around the next corner?

"I'm sure he'll be right back," Nick said. "We might as well get started." He walked to the nearest door. It had a narrow window next to it, but the glass was frosted, making it impossible to see through. He reached out and tried the door as the other kids watched with bated breath. The knob turned under his fingers and the door swung silently open a few inches.

"What do you see?" Angie asked, trying to peer around him.

Nick aimed his light through the opening, dreading what he might find.

Cody, who was tall enough to look over Nick's head, huffed. "It's just a plain old classroom."

Nick pushed the door the rest of the way open.

Frankenstein was right. After everything they'd seen outside, he'd expected to find something a little more exciting than rows of desks and a dusty chalkboard.

As the rest of the kids filed into the classroom, anticipation turned to disappointment. "It looks pretty much like our school," Dana said. "Except with less technology."

Cody picked up a pencil from a nearby desk. "See? Nothing here. Let's go."

"No one made you come," Angie said. "You can leave any time you want."

Tiffany opened a small closet near the back of the room, shined her light inside, and let out a piercing scream that set Nick's hair on end.

"What is it?" Dana called, rushing over.

Tiffany stumbled into a desk, her eyes wide. "A sk-sk-sk—" Her flashlight slipped from her fingers as she dropped into a chair.

Nick rushed over, looked into the closet, and gasped. A human skeleton stared back at him. There was no doubt about it this time. This wasn't someone's leftover dinner.

Angelo touched an arm bone and pulled it toward him. The skeleton rattled out of the dark. But a moment later, Angelo gave a disgusted sigh. "It's only a model."

"What?" Nick was sure they'd uncovered some terrifying secret. But Dana shined her flashlight on the skeleton and nodded her agreement.

"See the little metal hooks and strings holding it together? And the numbers on each of the bones? They use these to teach human anatomy."

"*This* is kind of odd," Angie said, flipping through a stack of textbooks.

"What is it?" Nick walked over to join her.

"Look at these titles." Angie turned the book and held her light so Nick could see the covers. *A Is for Apple*. She grabbed another one from a different stack. *Learning to Read*.

Cody shook his head. "What's the big deal? This is probably a kindergarten class."

"Maybe not." Angelo pointed his light at a glass jar of milky fluid with something pink floating in the middle. "Since when did six-year-olds start studying human brains?"

CHAPTER 13

YOU KNOW THAT MOMENT WHEN YOU REALIZE YOU AREN'T ALONE?

Nick aimed his flashlight into the glass container, creating a huge brain-shaped shadow on the blackboard behind it. "Maybe it's from a pig or something."

Dana dropped to one knee and stared at the brain floating in its milky bath. "Look at the size of those frontal lobes. It's definitely human."

"What's that liquid?" Angelo said, studying the glass container. "Normally organs would be preserved in a formalin solution or ethyl alcohol. This isn't either one. It looks more like some kind of nutrient broth." He tapped the side of the glass container and the brain moved slightly.

"Don't do that." Nick shuddered as the brain's shadow swayed back and forth on the blackboard. He had no idea what his friend was talking about, but the thought that he was looking at an actual human brain totally freaked him out.

"We should take this with us to study," Angelo said.

Cody stepped in front of him. "That's stealing. You agreed not to break any laws."

"If it belongs to one of the stolen bodies, it doesn't belong to Sumina Prep anyway," Nick said. "So how can it be stealing?"

Cody continued to stand in his way.

"Okay," Angelo said. "We won't take it. But I do want to get a closer look."

"A brain studying a brain," Tiffany said.

"What?" Angelo jerked the jar away from his face, bumping the table a little as he pulled away. "Is that supposed to be some kind of joke?" The jar teetered on the edge of the table, and for a moment it looked like the brain was going to fall off and crash to the ground. Nick and Dana both darted forward to steady it.

Tiffany swallowed. "Umm, sort of."

"How did you *do* that?" Angelo asked. His eyes were huge and he was breathing in short gasps.

Nick wondered if his friend had totally lost it. "Do

what? What are you talking about?"

Angelo looked at Nick and licked his lips. "Did you hear that?"

"The only thing I heard was Tiffany kidding around," Dana said, carefully. "What did *you* hear?"

Angelo rubbed his mouth with the back of his hand. "Nu-nothing." He backed away from the jar, staring at the brain as though he expected it to come after him. "I couldn't have heard anything if you guys didn't."

Nick looked at Angie, standing behind Angelo. She twirled a finger beside her head. "Maybe we should check out another room."

"Good idea," Nick said.

Grouped together, the six of them left the classroom. Nick wasn't sure what had happened back there, but whatever it was, something had completely freaked out Angelo. He kept glancing over his shoulder as they crowded through the door.

Nick looked down the dark hallway. How long had they been in the classroom? "Maybe we should check on Carter," he said.

But Angie was already trying the next door. "Look at this!" she called.

"Oh, wow!" Tiffany flipped open her camera phone and the flash blinded Nick as she took a picture.

Nick blinked, trying to get back his night vision. By the time he got to the door and could make anything out, the rest of the kids were already inside.

"It looks like an operating room," Dana said.

"I'll bet this is where they cut up the bodies." Angie waved her flashlight and Nick made out dozens of tables covered with white sheets. Beside each table was a metal tray filled with scalpels and other surgical equipment.

Lit only by a dim gas lamp, the room looked like it belonged in an old-fashioned hospital. But it didn't smell like a hospital. Nick wrinkled his nose. "It stinks in here. Like rotten meat or old fish."

"Totally rank," Tiffany agreed, waving her hands in front of her face. "I am never going to get this stench out of my hair."

"What are these?" Angelo pointed his light toward a counter covered with dozens of machines that sort of resembled what Angie's mom had in her lab. Nick reached toward one that looked like an extra-big ice-cream maker. But Angelo held out a hand. "Careful. We don't know what they do."

Dana picked up a plastic jug and squinted at the label. "Vasosol. I've never heard of it." She turned the jug around and read the back. "For the preservation and storage of human organs and tissues."

"They *are* the ones stealing the bodies," Angie said, slamming her fist into her palm. "I knew it."

"But why?" Nick asked. Clearly there was something bizarre going on here. But what was the point? Why would a private school go to all the trouble of stealing bodies and cutting them up or whatever it was they were doing when you could find out pretty much anything you wanted on the internet these days? Shoot, if you wanted to see a human brain all you had to do was find the medical channel on TV or go to YouTube.

"I think it's time to leave," Angelo said, licking his lips. "Whatever they're doing here, it's not normal medical procedures. I don't know what's going on. But I don't think they'd be happy to find us snooping around."

"I'm with Angelo," Cody said. "This place gives me a serious case of the creeps."

"Take some more pictures first," Angie said. "For evidence."

Tiffany snapped pictures of everything in sight. The flash from her camera made the operating tables stand out in sharp contrast. Nick felt like he was looking at a series of photographs from one of those old asylums where they cut out parts of people's brains or shocked them.

He edged closer to one of the tables and realized there was something hanging from the side. He lifted up a long, black nylon strap with Velcro on one end. Why would you need a strap to hold down dead people?

"That's it," he said, his heart pounding. "We're out of here." As he started for the door, it swung open.

Nick backed away as a figure appeared in the door, shining a light in his eyes. He held up his hands trying to see. "Wh-who's there?"

"There you are." Carter lowered his flashlight. "I've been looking all over for you guys." He grinned. "Isn't this place awesome?"

"Awesome?" Tiffany said. "Are you out of your tiny, sugar-addled mind? This place is a house of horrors. Have you even looked around?"

Carter rolled his eyes. "Only, like, half the school. You'd think there'd be bathrooms everywhere. I swear the kids in this place must all be walking around with their legs crossed trying to hold it."

"Now isn't the time for jokes," Nick said. He pointed his flashlight around the room. "Look at this place."

Carter waved his hand, like he was shooing away a fly. "This is nothing. You should see the electronics lab. Seriously, the coolest special-effects stuff you've ever seen. Spielberg could make movies there. Of course, by the time I found it, my kidneys were like, practically in my throat. Turns out the bathrooms are clear across the school. And get this, the toilets are these open holes with big old pipes beneath them. So I'm about to wet myself by the time I finally got there, and what do you think I saw?"

"Gross," Tiffany squealed. "That's just nasty."

"We don't want to hear about your bathroom activities," Dana said.

"My *what whats*?" Carter made a face. But it really was time to get out.

"Come on," Nick said. He started toward the only exit and froze. Slowly he raised his hand, the beam of his flashlight going from the floor, up Carter's body, and past his head.

"Oh. My. Gosh," Angie moaned.

Angelo's mouth dropped open.

Cody dropped to the floor and rolled under a bench.

Carter turned and looked up. Standing behind him, towering so tall that its head wouldn't quite fit through the doorway, was a terrifying creature huge enough to make Frankenstein look like a first-grader.

CHAPTER 14

IF YOUR SCHOOL IS ANYTHING LIKE THIS, CONSIDER A TRANSFER

Nick looked around the room for something to defend himself with. The only thing he could find was the kind of rubber hammer doctors tested your reflexes with. Even if it was ten times as big, there was no way it could stop the hulking creature bending down to look in through the doorway.

Angie reached into her pack and pulled out her pepper spray. Nick didn't think that was going to work either. The creature's shoulders were nearly as wide as a small car.

Cody backed against one of the carts, shaking so hard he rattled the surgical equipment.

"Get out of the way, Carter!" Dana yelled, swinging a metal bar she must have taken from one of the trays.

"What are you doing?" Carter shouted. "Leave my friend alone."

Nick thought Carter was yelling at the monster until he held out his arms, shielding the creature behind him.

"Your . . . *friend*?" Angelo asked.

"Of course," Carter said, as if it should have been obvious. "What did you *think* I saw in the bathroom?"

The creature opened its mouth wide, revealing a set of surprisingly white teeth, and made a *huck-huck* sound that Nick realized was laughter. "Is putting he the watering on the pantsies."

Carter looked at the front of his jeans, which had several spots, and flushed. "I kind of had a little accident. But you would too, if you were getting ready to go to the bathroom, when a giant suddenly asked, 'What be you doings?'"

The giant covered his mouth and giggled.

Nick lowered his hammer. "He's friendly?"

"Oh, yeah." Carter put a hand on the creature's knee which came nearly up to his waist. "Come in and say hi."

The giant had to duck and turn sideways to get through the door.

Dana shook her head. "He's huge. No wonder they won the football game."

Nick was sure this guy was even bigger than the Sumina Prep players he'd seen on the field Friday night. He was like some kind of freak of nature.

"Is fine timing to being . . ." The creature scratched the back of his head with a thick finger and paused before breaking into another wide grin. "To being greeting friendsies."

Despite his size, he didn't look much older than fifteen or sixteen. But beyond how big he was, there was something else odd about him Nick couldn't quite place. The giant held out his hand.

Nick hesitantly took it. He was sure the giant would crush his fingers to a bloody pulp, but his grip was surprisingly gentle. "Nice to meet you, um . . . " He looked to Carter, realizing he didn't know what to call the giant.

"He doesn't seem to be big on names," Carter said. "So I just call him Jake."

"Nice to meet you, Jake."

The giant grinned so wide, it looked like his face was going to split in half.

"Why does he talk like that?" Cody asked. He was no longer shaking now that he realized the creature wasn't a threat.

113

"He doesn't speak much English," Carter said. "I think maybe he's from Iceland or something."

"Iceland?" Dana asked skeptically. "What makes you think he's from Iceland?"

"You should feel his hands. Cold as ice. And look at the size of him. He's got to be from Russia."

"Iceland isn't *in* Russia," Angelo said, writing and drawing furiously in his journal.

"He looks kind of . . . um, lumpy," Angie said.

That's what he'd been missing, Nick thought. The lumpiness. Jake wasn't just big, he was misshapen, too. As if he'd worked out some parts of his body hard and others not at all. His chest was broad, but his arms were almost spindly. His legs were big, but his rear was absolutely huge. And he had odd bumps on his shoulders, knees, and other joints.

Jake's face drooped.

"Don't say that kind of stuff!" Carter hissed, livid with anger. "You hurt his feelings. How would you like it if someone said you looked lumpy?"

Tiffany walked cautiously forward and looked up into the giant's face. "Come down here where I can see you."

Jake knelt in front of her so that his face was only a little above her head. He sniffed. "Flowersies."

"At least someone likes my perfume," Tiffany said. She ran her fingers through the giant's thick black locks. "You have nice hair. But you're doing nothing with it. Let me see now."

Nick watched, amazed, as Tiffany rooted through her purse, pulling out a circular brush, a pick, and a small can of styling mousse. "Well, you've got lots of body. But whoever cuts your hair should be shot." She reached into her purse again, pulled out a small pair of scissors, and cut, brushed, and moussed, until even Nick had to admit Jake looked pretty good.

"What do you think?" Tiffany asked, holding up a compact.

Jake's eyes went wide as he looked at himself in the mirror. "Pret-ty," he crooned, clapping his plate-sized hands.

"Make sure to use a high-quality conditioner," Tiffany said, putting the mirror back in her purse. "Or those split ends will be back in no time."

The giant nodded, watching her with big, green puppy-dog eyes.

"Not to be a jerk or anything," Nick said, "but what exactly are we doing? We've gotta go back and tell the police what's happening here."

"Right," Cody agreed.

Carter eased up next to him and whispered, "What are you talking about?"

"These people are stealing dead bodies and cutting them up," Nick whispered back. "And your friend probably knows all about it."

Carter sniffed. "I'm sure Jake wouldn't have anything to do with something like that. Have you actually seen these so-called bodies?"

"We saw a brain," Angie said.

"And what do you think all this stuff is for?" Dana asked, pointing to the operating tables and surgical equipment. "You can't tell me he doesn't know."

Nick turned to Jake, who was still staring at Tiffany. "Do you know somebody called the Pale One?"

The giant immediately ducked his head and covered his face as though expecting to be hit. "Not are badding being," he cried, trembling. "No master seeing."

"You scared him." Carter rushed to Jake and hugged him—his arms going less than a third of the way around the giant's shoulders. "It's okay."

"I'm thinking he doesn't like the Pale One," Angelo said.

Nick nodded. If a guy this big was scared of the dude, he must be pretty nasty.

Outside, thunder crashed. Blue light flashed through the open door. Another crash came a moment later. And another blue flash. Jake buried his head in his hands and howled. "No-o-o-o-o."

"Guess he's not too crazy about the storm either," Angie said.

Dana titled her head, looking into the hallway outside the classroom. "How are we seeing lightning flash from inside the school when all the downstairs windows are covered?"

Angelo stuck his head through the door and glanced down the hallway. "There's something going on down that way," he said.

Nick followed him out of the classroom. At the far end of the hall a door was halfway open. Blue light flashed from the room, accompanied by a crashing sound they had taken for thunder.

"What is that?" Angie asked, coming up behind them.

Angelo shook his head. "An arc welder, maybe?"

Quietly, they crept down the hall. "It smells weird," Dana said. "Like some kind of chemicals."

They stopped just outside the door. Angelo eased it all the way open so they could look inside. He gasped and stepped back.

117

"What is it?" Nick asked, moving around to get a better look. Immediately he saw what had frightened Angelo.

Leaning over a table at the far end of the room was the Sumina football coach. Only he didn't look anything like a coach now. He was absolutely terrifying. Everything about him was white, from the wild hair that shot out from his head in every direction to his skin, which looked like it had never seen a day of sun. The only things not white were his pink eyes, which glowed like burning embers.

The man seemed to be performing some kind of operation. Nick could see a pair of legs sticking out from a white sheet. Blue bolts of electricity danced around the man's fingers, but Nick couldn't see any kind of equipment. It was almost like the man was creating the electricity himself. Sparks crackled from some sort of metal knobs at the sides of his jaws. His long white lab coat was stained with some dark liquid.

"What is that?" Angie said.

Nick didn't know, but all at once he wanted to get out. This was turning into way more than he had bargained for.

Cody elbowed his way forward. "That guy looks like some kind of mad scientist," he said.

At that moment the man moved and Nick could swear the legs were attached to nothing. Just above where the thighs should have been, the sheet lay flat on the table.

The Pale One looked toward the door as though he sensed someone was there. Nick backed away as the terrible pink eyes met his. The crazed man grinned at Nick and blue sparks shot out of his mouth.

At the same time, Dana yelled, "Run!"

Nick spun around to see a horde of hulking figures in football uniforms racing down the hallway toward them.

"We have visitors!" The mad scientist cackled. "Give them a special welcome."

Angelo grabbed Nick's arm. "We have to go."

Nick didn't need a second warning. "Out the door!" he yelled, pelting down the hall. In the dark it was hard to tell who was where. Bodies jostled against one another. People screamed. Nick felt a hand on his elbow and jerked away.

Something rammed into Angelo and his glasses flew from his face. He started to fall, but Nick grabbed his arms and pulled him forward. Then Nick was at the door, pushing, screaming, racing into the street as he felt the cold rain hit his face. He looked back to see

Angelo and Dana rush out the door. Angie was a few feet to their right. Carter sprinted past, catching up with Tiffany, who was in front of them all.

Because they didn't dare to look back for fear the football players were right behind them, it wasn't until they reached the train station at the bottom of the hill that they all stopped to catch their breath.

"I didn't see that," Carter repeated over and over. "I did *not* see that."

"It's not scientifically possible," Angelo muttered, squeezing his monster notebook until his fingers turned white.

"It has to be some kind of trick," Dana agreed. "Like in those haunted houses you see at Halloween. Or a movie effect of some kind."

Angie was standing with her hands on her knees, panting. "Whatever it was, at least we got away. We're all safe."

Nick looked around, taking a quick count, and his gut clenched in a hot ball of fear. "Not all of us," he whispered. "Cody's gone."

CHAPTER 15

RIGHT ABOUT NOW THEY SHOULD HAVE COME TO ME

"We have to go back," Nick said. Although the idea of going anywhere near the crazed man in the white lab coat made him want to puke his guts out, they couldn't leave Cody behind. Who knew what those freakazoids might do to him?

But Carter grabbed Nick's elbow as he turned to head up the hill. "Did you fry some brain cells in there? Going back to that school again is insane."

"For once, the mouth that eats all is right," Tiffany said.

Dana rubbed a bruise on her left arm she'd somehow gotten in their escape and chewed her lower lip.

"We don't know for *sure* that he's still in the school. Things were crazy. For all we know he turned a different direction than the rest of us. He might be heading for another train station right now. Or calling someone to get a ride."

The rain that had been falling all evening was finally coming to a stop, but the parking lot was filled with puddles. Nick stomped his foot in one, sending a spray of water onto a nearby car. "You're saying we leave him there? Am I the only one who saw what that crazy dude was doing in his lab?"

Angelo rubbed his eyes. He looked like a completely different person without his glasses. "If you want to go, I've got your back," he said to a parking meter.

"Over here." Nick sighed.

Angelo turned and squinted. "Oh, sorry."

Nick pressed his hands to his face. Of course they were right. Sneaking into the school had been crazy enough when no one was expecting them. If they tried it again now, they might as well be handing themselves over to the crazy dude with the pink eyes.

Cody might have forced his way into the group, and he might not be as close a friend as Carter, Angelo, or even the girls, but it still felt wrong to leave him there. "We could call the police," Angie suggested.

Nick took his hands from his eyes. "What would we say? We broke into a school and saw some crazy guy doing experiments on random body parts? They'd either throw us in jail or an insane asylum."

"We have proof," Angie said. "Tiffany's got pictures."

Tiffany fished around in her purse. "Oh, no," she moaned after several minutes of frantic looking. "I think I dropped my phone in the school. And it's got my name and address in it."

Dana checked her watch. "Whatever we're going to do, we have to decide quickly. The train will be here in a few minutes and my parents will ground me if I'm not home by ten."

Carter pointed to a pay phone. "We can make an anonymous call. Just say we saw some kid yelling for help at Sumina Prep. The police will check it out, discover what they're up to there, and rescue Frankenstein."

Nick nodded. That did sound like the best idea. "Who's going to make the call?"

"I will," Angie said. She went to the phone, picked up the receiver, and dialed 911 while the other kids crowded around her. "Hello?" she said, sounding breathless and panicked. "I just saw a boy screaming

123

for help outside Sumina Preparatory Academy. I think he might have been kidnapped." She gave a little sob that sounded completely believable.

And why not? They'd just seen something so terrifying, Nick was still trying to convince himself it couldn't have been real.

"My name?" Angie said into the phone. Angelo shook his head. "Kimber Tidwell. The boy who was screaming is Cody Gills, he goes to my school."

Carter chuckled. Kimber Tidwell was the most popular girl at their school and the only kid who cared more about fashion than Tiffany.

"Kimber Tidwell," Angie repeated. "T-I-D-W-E-L-L. My address? Why do you need to know my address? This happened at Sumina Prep." Overhead, the tracks began to rumble and the light of a train could be seen in the distance. Dana tugged Angie's jacket and pointed to her watch.

"I have to go," Angie said. "But please check on him right away. I think he's in danger. There's some weird stuff going on at that school. No. I'm sorry. I can't stay on the line."

"Let's go," Dana yelled as soon as Angie hung up the phone. The six of them raced up the stairs with Angelo clinging to Nick's shoulder for guidance. They reached the platform just in time to get onto the train before the doors closed.

"Are you sure it was a good idea to give them a real name?" Nick panted, dropping into his seat.

Angie took the seat across from him. "They wouldn't have taken me seriously if I didn't. And if Cody does end up missing, at least they'll know what school he goes to when they look up his name and Kimber's."

Nick pulled his knees up to his chest, wrapping his arms around his legs. Everything about this night had gone wrong. And even though Cody had beaten him up in the past more times than he could count, and was a total pain in the rear now, he couldn't help feeling like a coward for not going after him.

"It's going to be okay," Angelo said, patting him on the shoulder. "I'll bet Cody shows up tomorrow, making us promise to never do anything like that again."

But Cody wasn't at school the next day. Nick came up with several excuses to go to his classroom and every time he saw Cody's empty desk he felt more and more ill. At lunch the six of them went to the school's computer lab and searched for any news about Cody or Sumina Prep. But the only stories that came up for Sumina were about the game. There was no mention of Cody at all.

"Maybe he stayed home sick," Carter suggested as the six of them sat on the edge of the playground eating their lunches. "I know I had a pretty bad night."

"It doesn't seem to have affected your appetite," Angie said.

Carter screwed up his face, then stared longingly at Nick's orange cupcake. Nick ignored him. "I'm going to Cody's house after school to check on him."

"Technically, that might not be the best option," said Angelo, who was wearing a pair of tortoiseshell glasses with tinted lenses. Apparently his mother had purchased them for him a few months earlier, but he had refused to even try them on. Now they were his only choice until she could order him another pair. "If he *is* missing, it might look suspicious, you showing up at his house the very next day."

"So you want to do nothing? Pretend like last night never happened?" Nick slammed his fist on his lunch, mashing his cupcake into a smear of orange frosting and crumbs inside the plastic wrapper.

"Oh-h-h," Carter groaned. He picked up the flattened cupcake, turned it over in his hands, and said, "I think it's still edible."

"What choice do we have?" Angie asked. "If we tell anyone we broke into the school, we'll get in trouble.

And without Tiffany's pictures, we have no proof anything happened at all."

Tiffany, who looked completely lost without her phone, fiddled with her necklace. "The good news is the police haven't shown up asking any questions. And the school would be buzzing if anyone had contacted Kimber."

"All that means is the police didn't take our call seriously," Nick said. He watched Carter trying to suck cupcake crumbs out of the package and balled his fists. "Fine, I'll wait until tomorrow. If Cody isn't back by then, I'm going to his house. And if he's not there . . ." He wasn't sure what he'd do if Cody hadn't come home from Sumina Prep. But one thing he was sure of was that he couldn't just sit around and wait for word that something terrible had happened.

That night, all he could think about was Cody and what might be happening to him. As far as he had seen, they only experimented on dead bodies at Sumina. But what if that wasn't the case? What if right now, Frankenstein was strapped to a table while the Pale One shocked and probed him?

"Up for an episode of *Supernatural*?" his dad asked, turning on the TV. "I recorded it while you were at the game."

"I don't think so," Nick said. "Maybe I'll just go lie down."

Dad came over and put a hand on his head. "Give it to me straight. Are you dying of some rare tropical disease?"

"Huh?" Nick asked.

Dad plopped onto the couch beside him. "I've never seen you turn down the chance to watch a scary show. I taped it especially because I know how much you like it. So either you're dying, or there's something on your mind. Which is it?"

Nick wished he could tell his dad the truth. It would be so nice to confess to a grown-up and let them figure it out. But that would mean ratting on his friends. And even if his dad believed him, which wasn't likely, what could he do about it?

"It's the disease," Nick said, trying to give a convincing smile. "I've got two weeks to live. But don't worry. I left you my Tales from the Crypt comic-book collection."

He went up to his room before his dad could ask him any more questions. But he didn't sleep well that night. And when Cody wasn't in class the next morning, he made his decision.

"I'm going," he told the other kids at the first recess.

Carter gulped, his Adam's apple bobbing up and down. "I'll go too."

Angelo pushed his glasses up on his nose. "I'll go."

Angie looked at Dana and Tiffany, who nodded. "Okay. We're in."

CHAPTER 16

THIS IS WHY YOU SHOULD NEVER JUDGE A BOOK BY ITS COVER. EXCEPT FOR THIS BOOK, WHICH HAS A REALLY AMAZING COVER

Nick walked along the sidewalk with his head down. Frankenstein's house had always been a place kids avoided at all costs and here he was walking straight to it. He wasn't sure what he'd say when he reached it. What if the police were there? After two days of Cody being missing, someone must have called them.

"Your mom still hasn't got you the new glasses, huh?" Carter asked Angelo.

Angelo shook his head. "She requested them, but the lenses won't be ready until Friday. They're special order."

"I like these ones," Tiffany said. "They give you a Justin Bieber vibe."

Carter chortled and started singing in a completely off-key voice. "You know you love me, I know you ca-air-air. Cause I have stinky underwear-r-r-r."

Tiffany frowned. "That's not the way it goes."

"It should," Carter said. "When I'm a famous musician, all of my songs will include underwear, farting, and the occasional armpit noise."

"If you're ever a famous musician," Tiffany said, "I'm going have to my ears permanently sealed closed."

Carter grinned. "All the more reason."

Even Carter's joking couldn't shake Nick from the funk he was in.

"It's not your fault," Angie said.

Nick grunted and turned away.

Angie moved to stand in front of him. "It's not any of our faults. We didn't ask him to come with us. We called the police. What more could we have done?"

A couple of little kids zipped by on scooters, pretending to shoot each other with squirt guns. How would it feel to have your biggest worry in the world be whether to watch Nickelodeon or the Cartoon Network? "We could have gone back for him," he muttered.

"Then we'd all be wherever he is," Angie said. "Is

that what you want?"

Nick gritted his teeth. He didn't know what he wanted. Angie was probably right. What chance did six kids have against whatever lived in that school, or castle, or whatever it was? Running had been their only choice. So why did he feel like crap?

"What do you think he was doing in there?" he asked. "In that lab, with the electricity?"

"No clue," Angie said.

Nick wondered if she'd seen what he thought he'd seen. But the idea of a leg walking by itself was too crazy to consider. Obviously it was some kind of trick. Or maybe he'd seen it from a bad angle. Since no one else had mentioned it, he figured he must have been the only one.

Cody lived in a small one-story house with peeling metal siding. The front lawn was mowed almost to the dirt, which seemed sort of pointless since it looked like it was mostly weeds. A tiny dog with a face like a rat jumped off the porch and started yapping at the kids as they started up the walkway.

Carter ran toward it waving his arms and yelled, "Boogetta, boogetta, boogetta." The dog skidded to a halt, yelped, and retreated around the side of the house.

"I see you're as good with animals as you are with people," Tiffany said.

"Pretty much," Carter said, either missing her sarcasm or choosing to ignore it. "I'm kind of like a dog whisperer. Only in reverse."

Nick was working up the courage to approach the porch when the front door flew open and an old man in baggy pants and a dirty T-shirt peered out. "Who's bothering my dog?" he shouted.

Carter started whistling his underwear song and pretended to study the lawn.

"We were looking for Frank—" Nick started before realizing what he'd almost said. "Umm, Cody."

The old man put a hand to one of his large, wrinkled ears. "Frank Cody, you say? Don't know no Frank Cody."

"He means Cody Gills," Angie said, stepping up beside him. Nick was grateful for her help. "Is he home?"

The old man's upper lip curled, revealing a set of clearly false teeth. "Who's asking?"

Nick looked to Angie and she rolled her eyes. If this was Cody's dad, no wonder he was angry all the time. "Umm, us?" he ventured.

The man scratched his chin like he was thinking

that over. Although what little hair he had on his head was white, the long scraggly whiskers poking out from his chin were red. "He ain't here," he said at last. He gave his sagging pants a yank and turned to walk back into the house.

"Wait!" Nick called.

The man turned halfway around in the doorway as if he wasn't sure whether it was worth his time to come out again or not.

Dana quickly walked up, holding out her hand. "I'm Dana Lyon," she said, smiling broadly.

She was about six inches taller than the man, and he looked her up and down dubiously. "Big old bean plant, ain't you?"

"I guess," Dana said, trying to keep the smile on her face. "Are you Cody's father?"

"Grandfather," the man snapped. "On his mother's side. He stole your bike or roughed you up, I don't want to hear about it. Boy's never been nothing but trouble."

"What's he done now?" a voice shouted from inside the house. "If it's the police, tell them to throw him in jail and toss away the key."

So many things about Cody began to make sense. No wonder he was always prowling around the

134

neighborhood. Who'd want to live with people like this? "He didn't take our bikes and he didn't . . . *rough us up*," Nick said.

"At least not lately," Carter mumbled, and Nick shot him a warning look.

"We just haven't seen him at school and we wanted to make sure he's okay. We're kind of his friends," Nick said. It wasn't totally a lie, either. As much of a pain as Cody was, Nick had sort of gotten used to him. He thought Carter and Angelo might feel the same way, although they'd never actually discussed it.

"*Friends*?" the old man asked, as though he'd never heard the word before. He narrowed his eyes. "Since when does that troublemaker have friends?"

"If it's the school," the voice from the inside of the house shrilled, "tell them we haven't seen him!"

"He isn't a troublemaker anymore. He's changed," Angelo said. "Have you even called the police to report that he's missing?"

The old man tugged at one of his long red whiskers and scowled at Angelo's glasses. "Who are you supposed to be? Some kind of motion picture star?"

Angelo's face went red.

"No. I ain't called the police and I ain't going to,"

135

the old man said. "I'd imagine they're as glad to be rid of him as I am. Once a troublemaker, always a troublemaker. Probably went back to live with his father. Two of 'em deserve each other." With that, he yanked up his pants again, walked into the house, and slammed the door behind him.

"Wow," Nick said as the kids turned and walked back to the street. "Can you believe those two?"

"I can't believe they haven't noticed how different he is," Dana said.

Angelo scratched his head. "It explains why the police haven't come looking for him."

"I have to get home," Tiffany said. "My parents are still mad that I lost my phone. They're saying they might not get me another one till after Christmas."

"I've gotta go too," Dana said. "My cousins are coming for Thanksgiving and I'm supposed to help clean the house."

Angie kicked a rock into the gutter. "I'm sorry I suggested we go to the school," she said quietly.

Nick shrugged. "It isn't your fault. We'd have gone with or without you."

Angie snorted. "A bunch of chickens like you three? I don't think so."

Normally Nick enjoyed a good argument with Angie. But right now his heart just wasn't in it.

"Well, see you around," Angie said.

"See you." They had the next three days off school for fall break, and there didn't seem to be much else they could do about the body snatching.

"Want to go play some Left 4 Dead 2?" Angelo asked.

"I guess," Nick said as the three of them walked down the street.

"Let's go to your house," Carter said hopefully. "Maybe your mom's baking something."

The next three hours were a blur of chopping, shooting, and exploding the infected zombie creatures. But even that didn't cheer Nick up.

"Are you *trying* to get us killed?" Carter asked when Nick's inattention caused them to be overrun by the bloodthirsty hordes for the third time in an hour.

Nick sighed and dropped his controller. "Sorry," he muttered. "My heart just isn't in it. I keep thinking about Cody spending Thanksgiving getting shock treatments or locked in a cold cell or something."

"Well look who's here," Nick's dad called out in a cheerful voice as he came through the front door

137

that evening. "It's Nick the Nerd and his sidekicks the Smarticle Particle and the Mouth from the South."

"Hi, Dad," Nick said. His father was taking off Wednesday to give himself a five-day weekend and was looking forward to trying out his new P40 WarHawk remote-controlled plane.

"Have you eaten me out of house and home yet?" Dad asked, kicking off his shoes and dropping into a recliner.

"Only house," Carter said. "I plan on coming by Thursday after we get back from my grandma's to finish the home part."

Nick looked from the video game to his dad, and finally made the decision he'd been considering for the last two days.

Angelo seemed to sense what Nick was thinking and shook his head. "Not a good idea," he whispered.

But Nick had made up his mind. Before he could talk himself out of it, he opened his mouth and blurted, "Dad, Sunday night we snuck into Sumina Prep. We thought they were stealing bodies and it turns out they are. There's this crazy guy who is doing some weird experiments, and a human brain in a jar, and this giant who doesn't speak much English, and these operating tables with straps to hold people down."

Dad blinked. Carefully he loosened his badly tied necktie and folded his arms. His face was so still Nick couldn't tell what his father was thinking. "Anything else?"

Nick wiped his eyes, which were suddenly wet. "They kidnapped Cody Gills."

CHAPTER 17

I'M CERTAIN THE GROWN-UPS WILL HAVE THIS CLEARED UP IN NO TIME

"Who do you think he's talking to?" Carter whispered. He, Nick, and Angelo had been waiting in Nick's room while Mom and Dad spoke in the kitchen. They'd heard Nick's dad make several phone calls over the last half hour. But with the door closed, it was impossible to hear what he was saying or who he was saying it to.

"The police?" Angelo suggested.

"Probably our parents," Carter said.

Nick felt terrible for getting his friends in trouble and he appreciated the fact that they'd both agreed to stick with him. "I'm sorry, guys," he said.

"Don't be sorry." Angelo patted him on shoulder. "It

was the right thing to do. You were just the only one brave enough to do it."

Carter folded and unfolded an empty package of Chips Ahoy! cookies. "Couldn't you have waited until after the holidays though? I hate being grounded on vacation."

Nick and Angelo looked at him, and he threw the wrapper toward the trash can, missing by at least a foot. "Okay, that was selfish."

Angelo tapped his pen on a page of his monster notebook, not writing anything. "I noticed you didn't mention the girls."

Nick nodded. "No point getting them into trouble too."

Footsteps sounded in the hallway and the three boys looked up as the bedroom door swung open. "Come into the living room," Dad said. "Your mom and I need to talk with you."

Nick led his friends out of his room, thinking he'd never felt less like one of the Three Monsterteers. As they shuffled over to the couch, he snuck a peek at his mom. She was sitting with her back board-straight, her mouth a thin white line. This was not going to go well.

Dad stood with his arms folded across his chest and waited until all three boys met his eyes. "First of all,

I want to say that I expected more out of the three of you."

"It's not just the lying about where you were Sunday night or the trespassing," Mom said sternly. "Although those are bad enough. But waiting this long to tell us about it when one of your friends could be in danger is completely unacceptable."

"I thought I could trust you," Dad said. Nick wilted at the disappointment in his father's voice and in his eyes.

"Nick wanted to tell you sooner," Angelo said. "But I wouldn't let him."

"I wouldn't either," Carter said. "And if it helps, I've totally lost my appetite. Right before Thanksgiving, too."

"Did you find out if Cody is all right?" Nick asked. He didn't care if he got grounded for a month as long as Cody was found safe.

Dad rubbed a finger across the skin between his nose and his upper lip. "His grandparents seem to believe he's with his father because he's afraid of getting into trouble for breaking into the school."

"But that's not—" Nick began.

His father held up a finger. "I'm only repeating what they told me."

"Are the police at least looking for him?" Nick asked.

"At this time they have no reason to believe he is a missing person."

"Of course he's a missing person," Nick said. He couldn't believe his dad was buying the garbage Cody's grandparents were giving. "Didn't you listen to anything I said about the school? There's something totally messed up going on there. That guy's stealing corpses and now he's got Cody. I know it."

Mom stood up and glared at him. "I am *this* close to throwing every monster comic book, movie, game, and model you own in the trash," she said, holding her thumb and forefinger less than an inch apart.

Angelo gasped.

"The only reason I haven't," she continued, "is because I know how much you boys care about them. You're just lucky the police aren't charging you with breaking and entering."

"Sorry," Nick muttered. He couldn't believe his own mom and dad were more concerned about what they had done at the school than they were about a kidnapping.

"You can say just how sorry you are tomorrow," Dad said.

Nick tensed. "What do you mean?"

143

Dad smiled for the first time during their entire conversation and Nick didn't like the look of it.

"He means you will have the chance to say you're sorry in person," Mom said, "when your father takes you to Sumina Preparatory Academy in the morning to apologize to Mr. Dippel, the Sumina headmaster, face-to-face."

Angelo and Carter looked at Nick like he'd just been given a death sentence.

"As for the two of you," Mom said, "we have *not* told your parents."

Carter gave a huge sigh of relief. "Thank you. Thank you. Thank you. Mr. and Mrs. B, you guys are the best."

Dad smiled again. "*We* have not told them because *you* will tell them yourselves. Between now and tomorrow morning when I pick you up to apologize with Nick."

• • •

Wednesday morning, the three boys huddled in the backseat of the Braithwaites' SUV, dreading their return visit to the Sumina building.

"Did you tell your dad the guy's crazy?" Carter whispered.

"He won't listen. He thinks there's a rational explanation." Nick sighed. His dad had no imagination. If there was a zombie apocalypse, his dad would be the first one infected, because he'd be looking for the zippers on the backs of the costumes when the horde attacked.

When Carter got nervous he ate even more than usual. This morning, he had an entire package of Oreos shoved down the front of his coat, and he was going through the cookies like he had to finish them all before they reached the school. "What if he kidnaps us?" he said, spraying crumbs.

"That won't happen," Angelo said. "He couldn't afford the publicity if we disappeared too."

"That'll be good to know when those goons of his grab us and take us into his dungeon. When the mad scientist is hooking electrodes to your head you can tell him what bad publicity that is." Carter shoved four cookies in his mouth at the same time, turning his teeth a disgusting shade of black.

"Want some music?" Dad asked. "I've got *Johnny Horton's Greatest Hits*." He started humming, "Sink the Bismarck." "La-dee-dee da-dee-dee 'cause the world depends on us."

"No thanks," all three boys said at once.

"You should ask him if he's got 'It's the End of the World as We Know It,'" Carter said.

"You know, it's a funny thing," Dad said, trying to hum and talk at the same time. "I called a friend of mine in the Diablo Valley Police Department. He said they haven't had any problems with Sumina Prep. But they *did* get a 911 call Sunday night from someone claiming to be a girl who goes to your school."

Nick held his breath.

"But when they called her house, it turned out the girl wasn't anywhere near Diablo Valley that night, so they put it down as a prank call. But you wouldn't know anything about that since it was just three of you *boys* out at the school, right?"

The three friends glanced uncomfortably at each other. "Actually, that Johnny Horton's sounding pretty good right about now," Carter said.

When they pulled up in front of the school, Nick noticed something different right away. "The shutters are open."

Dad glanced out his window and squinted at the thick wooden shutters that had been closed tight before. "Wasn't there a pretty good storm Sunday night? They were probably worried the high winds would break the glass."

Nick knew it couldn't be anything that innocent, but he kept his mouth shut.

"Quite a place," Dad said when they got out of the car. He craned his head back to see the top story. "Hard to believe it's only been here for a little over a year."

"That's not possible," Nick said. "These stones have to be at least a hundred years old."

"Actually closer to nine hundred," a voice said. Nick turned to see the mad scientist standing casually outside the door to the school. Without his lab coat, and with no electricity sparking from his fingertips, he looked more like a football coach again. But his flour-white skin, pink eyes, and crazy white hair still terrified Nick. He pressed back against his dad.

"Considering that the oldest surviving building in California is Mission San Juan Capistrano, which was built in 1776, this can't be nine hundred years old," Angelo said. Nick was impressed that his friend could even talk. His throat felt like he'd swallowed a handful of sand.

The headmaster gave a wheezy laugh that freaked Nick out. Even standing beside his dad in the middle of the day the guy was seriously eerie. All the more so when you knew he had Cody hidden away some-where. "This one is too smart for his own good," he said with a strange accent Nick couldn't place. All of his s's sounded like z's, his w's and f's sounded like v's, and his

147

d's sounded like t's. "This castle was built by one of my long dead ancestors. It was rather famous until it fell into disrepair. I had it shipped here and reassembled stone by stone."

"That must have cost a small fortune," Nick's father said. He held out his hand. "Daniel Braithwaite." Nick wanted to warn him about the electricity, but managed to bite his tongue.

"Dr. Franz Dippel." The pale man shook Mr. Braithwaite's hand, and Nick was surprised to see there wasn't so much as a spark. Maybe he could turn the power off and on. "And these must be the miscreants who broke into my school." He turned his pink eyes on Nick, Carter, and Angelo. "I must say, you gave my students and me quite a scare," he said with another wheezy laugh.

"*You?*" Carter sputtered. "We scared *you*? When I saw you shocking that body in your lab, my teeth chattered so hard, I sounded like a woodpecker."

The headmaster's eyes narrowed for a moment, his face hardening into an expression that looked much closer to what Nick remembered from Sunday night. The expression disappeared so quickly Nick wondered if his dad had even seen it. When he turned to check, he saw that his father was frowning at Carter. "My son and his friends seem to think they saw something strange happening in your school," he said. "But that's not why we're here, is it boys?"

"No," Nick mumbled. "We're here to say we're sorry for trespassing in your school."

"I'm sorry," Angelo said. "We shouldn't have nosed around."

"Yeah. I'm sorry too." Carter rubbed a hand across his jacket and Nick was pretty sure he was checking on his cookies.

"Well," Dr. Dippel said with a smile that looked totally fake to Nick, "no harm done." He reached into the pocket of his suit, which looked like something a man might have worn in Europe in the 1800s, and pulled out a pair of glasses with one broken lens. "Do these belong to one of you?"

Angelo eased forward. "They're mine." Nick could have sworn the doctor smirked as Angelo took his glasses while being careful not to touch the headmaster's fingers.

"Why don't you let me take you on a tour of the school?" Dr. Dippel suggested. "Perhaps things will look at little less 'strange,' as you say, in the light of day."

Nick glanced at Angelo. How could the headmaster

149

let them inside the school knowing what they would see?

"No way," Carter whispered. "If we go in, we'll never come out."

"Would you boys like that?" Mr. Braithwaite asked.

Nick drew a deep breath. This was his chance to show his dad what they'd seen Sunday night. And maybe they could figure out where the headmaster had taken Cody. Unless Carter was right and it was some sort of trap.

"Let's go in," Angelo said.

"Okay," Nick agreed.

"Come, come." Dr. Dippel held open the front door. As Nick entered the school, he felt like he was walking into a nightmare.

"Over there," Nick said, pointing to the first door they had entered Sunday night.

"Of course," the headmaster said. "Go anywhere you like."

He was sure that the brain would be gone. But it was still on the table. "See," Nick hissed to his dad.

Mr. Braithwaite leaned over to look in the jar. "Is this real?" he asked like a kid in a candy shop.

"Yes, of course," the headmaster said in his strange accent. "Most schools have only pig or cow brains to

150

study in anatomy class. This was a gift to the academy from a good friend at a large university in London."

"That is so-o-o cool," Mr. Braithwaite said.

Nick couldn't believe his dad was that gullible. Didn't he understand this brain hadn't come from London, but had been stolen from a cemetery or hospital right in their own hometown? "How do you explain the kids' books?" he demanded. "Don't tell me you have little kids learning how to read and studying brains at the same time." Let him explain his way out of that.

Dr. Dippel steepled his fingers in front of his face. "I am afraid my students are not from America. In their home country they are very advanced. In English, they must learn, as you say, like the little children."

"I want to ask them some questions," Carter said. "Especially Jake."

The headmaster stuck out his lower lip. "Jake?"

"You know. Seven feet tall. Wide as a dump truck," Carter said. "He's kind of hard to miss."

"Ahhh." Dr. Dippel smiled. "Boleslav. A large boy to be sure. I am afraid he, along with all my other students, have gone home for the break."

"And where would that be?" Nick asked.

Dr. Dippel smiled even wider. "Transnistria. You have heard of it?"

Nick hadn't. Even Angelo seemed unsure. "Is it somewhere near Ukraine?" he asked.

"Very good," the headmaster said, with a clap of his pale hands. "What would you like to see now?"

Nick had a feeling Dippel would have an excuse for everything. And sure enough, the operating tables were for dissecting frogs and snakes. The lab where they'd seen blue fire was for advanced electronics. Even the body they'd seen on the table was nothing more than a robot the kids had been working on as a school project.

The headmaster led them through every room in the school. There were no hidden dungeons or cells. Nothing that looked even slightly questionable or dangerous. By the end, Nick was beginning to think they'd made a mistake.

"If you don't mind my asking," Nick's dad said when they returned to the front of the school. "What happened to your jaw?"

Mr. Dippel touched the bolts on either side of his face. "War of Transnistria. A terrible thing. A bullet went from one side to the other, shattering my jaw and cheekbones in many places. The physicians placed screws to hold in place. Now I must eat much of, what is it you say here? Jell-O, I think?"

"I'm sorry to hear that," Nick's dad said. "And I think

152

we've learned a valuable lesson. Not to judge people who are different from us. Don't you agree, boys?"

Nick and his friends nodded.

Dr. Dippel laughed his odd little laugh. "And I will remember to lock my doors."

CHAPTER 18

OR NOT

Thanksgiving was usually one of Nick's favorite holidays. It didn't have the gifts of Christmas or the costumes of Halloween—which was his all-time favorite holiday—but it had lots of good food, no school, and great parades on TV.

This year, though, all he could think about was Cody. It was crazy how you could go from fearing someone to worrying about them in less than a week. But that's exactly what had happened. He phoned the bully's house so many times Cody's grandfather threatened to call the police if he heard from him again.

"I'm sure he'll come back once he realizes Dr. Dippel isn't going to press charges for breaking into his school," Dad said.

"I hope so." Nick poked listlessly at a turkey leg. But inside he knew that wasn't going to happen. Nick had no doubt something bad had happened to Cody. But there was nothing he could do about it except check the news and worry.

Finally his parents got so sick of him moping about the house that they ungrounded him, with the provision that he not go anywhere near Sumina Prep. That wasn't a problem. Nick had no desire to even see that building again. While the headmaster appeared to have explained everything away, Nick still had a strong feeling there was more to the school—and the doctor—than met the eye. But he had no proof.

Angelo's mom must have felt the same way as Nick's parents, because Friday afternoon, Angelo called to say he was no longer grounded. "You want to meet at the library?" he said. "Since it's still raining outside and all."

Nick wasn't fooled by his friend's casual attitude for a minute. "You want to go see Mr. Blackham, don't you?" Bartholomew Blackham was a reference librarian with an open mind and an unusually broad knowledge of the supernatural. He'd helped the boys out before, when Nick turned into a zombie.

"Well," Angelo admitted, "I *have* been doing a little research while I've been stuck at home. And I think Mr. Blackham might be able to answer some questions for us."

"Awesome," Nick said, feeling a slight ray of hope for the first time in days. "What about Carter? Do you think his parents will let him leave the house?"

"Are you kidding? He's driving them crazy, bugging his sisters and fighting with his little brother. They'd probably pay him to go." Angelo paused. "Would it be okay if I invited the girls too?"

"Totally. The more brains we have working on this the better." As soon as he hung up the phone Nick grabbed his coat and backpack and headed for the door. "I'm going to the library," he called on his way out.

"Have a good time," his mom said, looking up from her crossword puzzle. "And find something to read that *isn't* about monsters."

"I'd recommend *Gone with the Wind*. Or possibly *Little Women*," Dad said from the table, where he was examining the remains of his plane he'd crashed on its first flight. "The only thing better than a good tornado story is one about undersized female wrestlers."

Mom wrinkled her nose and Nick laughed. Closing the door behind him, he pulled his jacket over his head

156

as he ran to get his bike. By the time he reached the library, Angelo and Carter were waiting for him in the lobby. Angelo was wearing his long black coat again and for the first time Nick recognized how much it looked like the one Mr. Blackham had been wearing the last time they saw him. Maybe Angelo had chosen it for that reason.

"Did you bring any leftovers?" Carter asked, eyeing Nick's backpack. "I could really go for a cold turkey sandwich with cranberry sauce."

Nick rolled his eyes. "Oh, yeah. I always bring leftovers to the library with me."

A few minutes later, Angie, Tiffany, and Dana strolled through the front doors. Nick wondered if they'd all been together when Angelo called or if they just planned to make their entrances at the same time.

"Any word from Cody?" Dana asked.

"Nothing," Nick said. "And the police still aren't doing anything about it."

"I can't believe his grandparents aren't even worried," Tiffany said. "It makes me want to go over there and whack them both upside the head."

Angie turned to Nick. "I heard you told your dad about what happened."

Nick tapped his foot on the floor, leaving wet shoe

157

prints on the lobby carpet. "It was probably dumb."

"Actually," Angie said, "it was probably the smartest thing any of us have done since this whole thing happened. But thanks for not telling about us. My mom would have grounded me forever if she knew why we were really at the mortuary."

Nick shrugged, feeling suddenly embarrassed. "It's no big deal . . ."

"Are we just going to stand around?" Angelo tapped his notebook against his legs. "I want to see what Mr. Blackham has to say about all of this. He must have heard about the stolen bodies."

"Yeah. I want to meet this mystery man," Dana said. "I've been to this library hundreds of times and I've never heard of any Mr. Blackham."

Carter laughed. "You'd remember if you saw him. He looks kind of like an older Neo from *The Matrix.*"

But when they headed toward the back of the library, where Mr. Blackham worked, a gray-haired woman stopped them at the reference desk. "Can I help you?"

"We're here to see Mr. Blackham," Angelo said.

"I'm afraid he's not here." The woman examined a book, wrote something on a paper, and placed the book on a rolling cart. "Why don't you try again next week?

He should be back by them."

"This is kind of important," Nick said. "Do you have a number we can reach him at?"

The librarian picked up another book, then spotted a tear in one of the pages and clucked. "I'm afraid he's out of the country. Some sort of last-minute trip."

Nick frowned. Next week could be too late for Cody.

"Is there something I could help you with?" the librarian asked.

"I don't think so," Angelo said. "This is the kind of problem only he knows about."

The woman put down her book and really looked at the six of them for the first time. "Was he expecting you?"

"I don't see how he could have been," Nick said. "We didn't decide to come here until this morning."

She patted her hair. "Because he did call the day after he left on his trip. The connection was terrible. It sounded like he was calling from the middle of nowhere. But I believe he said something about some girls and boys coming to see him."

Angelo perked up. "What did he say?"

The librarian poked around her desk, searching through scraps of paper. "I thought I wrote it down somewhere. But I don't see it." She looked at Angie and her friends. "Is one of you named Shelly, by any chance?"

Angie shook her head.

"How about Mary? The static on the line was horrible, but I thought he mentioned two girls named Shelly and Mary."

"That's not us," Tiffany said. "There are a couple of girls named Shelly at our school. But I don't know anyone named Mary."

The woman continued to look around her desk, although Nick was pretty sure she was just turning over the same papers she'd already looked at. "Well, I guess it's not you then. I'm quite sure he mentioned a Shelly, a Mary . . . and possibly a Calvin?" She smiled at Angelo. "You wouldn't be Calvin, would you? You look like a Calvin."

"No, sorry," Angelo said.

Dejected, the six of them walked back to a circular table and took off their coats.

"I was really hoping he might have been able to help us," Angelo said, sliding into a chair.

"You think he would have believed any of it?" Angie asked. "I can't imagine anyone who wasn't at the school that night accepting what we saw. Especially not a grown-up."

"This dude's not like any grown-up I've ever met," Carter said. "He's actually a little freaky himself."

Nick scratched his head. It was going to be a long weekend. "What was that you were saying on the phone about research?" he asked Angelo.

"Nothing all that helpful at this point. There are just a few things that don't add up." Angelo pushed his glasses up on his nose and squinted at his notebook. "First, the screws in Dr. Dippel's jaw."

"The ones electricity was sparking from?" Tiffany shuddered. "Those freaked me out."

"Well, he said they were from the Transnistrian war. But the only Transnistrian war I could find was fought twenty years ago. He looks a little old to have been a soldier back then."

"Sometimes countries recruit anyone who can carry a gun," Dana said. "Especially smaller countries."

Angelo nodded. "That's true. But I also couldn't find any medical procedure that left screws poking out through the skin on a patient's jaw no matter how badly broken it might have been. Then there's the cas-tle—the one he said his ancestors built. I could swear I've seen that castle somewhere before. But I searched castles from Transnistria and there's nothing that looks remotely like it."

"It was a good thought," Nick said. "But he didn't actually say the castle itself was from Transnistria."

"I know," Angelo said, clenching his pen in his fist. "That's why I wanted to talk to Mr. Blackham. I was hoping he might know more about the building. He's something of a European history buff. Then there's the thing with the wires. I noticed it the first night we were there and again yesterday. There are enough wires going into that school to power a building ten times its size. Why do they need so much power?"

Carter gnawed on a stale-looking Crunch bar he'd produced from one of his pockets. "Especially when all the lights are gas."

"Wait a minute," Nick said. And everyone at the table turned to look at him.

"What is it?" Angie asked.

He wasn't sure. Something about castles and electricity had clicked inside his head. But there was something else. "My mom told me to get a book. But one that wasn't about monsters."

Dana waved a hand at the shelves and shelves of books surrounding them. "You have plenty of choices."

Nick closed his eyes, trying to focus. The librarian said Mr. Blackham mentioned two girls named Shelly and Mary. Why did those names sound so familiar?

And why did the idea of a castle and electricity make him think about what his mom had said. Separately they didn't mean anything, but together . . .

Suddenly his eyes snapped open. "I've got it!" He raced into the fiction section that was organized by the last names of the authors, and ran to the S's, ignoring the dirty looks shot at him by several adults.

Sherman, Sheehan, Sheldon, there it was. He grabbed a paperback with a man standing in front of icy mountains on the cover and hurried back to the table. It was exactly the kind of book his mother had asked him *not* to get.

"It wasn't Shelly and Mary," he said. "It was Mary Shelley." That was an author any self-respecting monster lover knew and every eye at the table opened wide with recognition.

Nick slapped the book on the table with a bang that echoed through the library. It was *Frankenstein*, by Mary Shelley. "Mr. Blackham wasn't talking about girls. He was talking about Frankenstein."

CHAPTER 19

I WAS REALLY STARTING TO WONDER IF I'D OVERESTIMATED THEM

Angelo slapped himself in the middle of the forehead like a cartoon character who'd just had a great idea. "Of course. Frankenstein!"

Dana appeared a little embarrassed that she hadn't thought of it first. She tapped her fingers on the table. "You know, if Mary and Shelly weren't girls' names, maybe Calvin wasn't a boy's name. In fact, maybe Mr. Blackham didn't say *Calvin* at all."

Angelo's eyes lit up. "The librarian said there was a lot of static on the line, so she might have misheard. Maybe he actually said *Galvan*. Are you thinking what I'm thinking?"

"Absolutely." Dana jumped up. "I'll go get a book on scientists from the 1700s and 1800s." She hurried into the nonfiction section of the library.

"I don't get it," Carter said. "What's the big deal about some old monster book? Frankenstein wasn't even all that cool of a monster. The mummy was way better."

"Frankenstein wasn't the monster," Angie said. "He was the scientist."

"Exactly." Angelo picked up the book from the table. "In Mary Shelley's story, Frankenstein was a mad scientist trying to discover the secret of life."

It was all starting to make more sense to Nick. "You think Mr. Blackham was trying to give us some kind of message? You think he knew about Dippel?"

Angelo flipped through the last few pages of his notebook. "I think he knew about Dippel and he was trying to tell us what he was up to at the school. It definitely explains all the power cables running into the building."

Angie held out her hands. "Wait just a minute. What does any of this have to with Calvin or Galvan?"

"Luigi Galvani," Dana said, returning from her search. She laid a heavy book on the library table and turned it around so the rest of them could see a picture of a man in a white wig.

Carter looked at the picture and snorted. "He looks kind of like George Washington. Wasn't he, like, the sixth president of the United States, or something?"

"Galvani wasn't a politician," Dana said. "He was one of the first scientists to study bioelectricity and he was a pioneer in the field of neuroelectrophysiology."

"I hope the rest of you got that. Because it went straight over my head," Tiffany said, holding her palm about a foot over the top of her perfect hair. "Give this to us in sixth-grade terms. Or in Carter's case, maybe third grade."

Carter made a face. "I may not be a brain. But at least I'm not a pioneer in neuro-ugly-ology like you."

Dana turned to Angelo, who was so anxious to talk he was bouncing in his seat. "Go ahead and explain it to them," she said.

Angelo leaned forward and took a deep breath like a teacher about to give a lecture. "Okay, so back in the 1700s scientists didn't know what caused muscle movement. Most of them thought it was controlled by air or blood flow. This was called the balloonist theory, popular with . . ."

Nick spun his finger in a "let's get on with it" gesture.

Angelo blinked, then bobbed his head. "Right. Anyway, back to Galvani. He was doing this experiment with a frog and static electricity when his assistant accidentally touched a charged scalpel to the leg of a skinned frog. When the electricity touched the dead frog's muscle, bam! It moved." He waved his hands excitedly. "That's how they discovered that electricity, in the form of ions, is what causes muscles to contract. The theory became known as galvanism, which we now call neuroelectrophysiology."

Carter opened his mouth in a huge fake yawn. "This is fascinating stuff, and I'm, like, totally excited to be spending one of my last vacation days learning science. But, um, so what?"

Angelo looked offended. "So what is that a lot of other scientists at that time did more tests using galvanism. Including on corpses. Some of them believed a dead person could be brought back to life by shocking the body. A lot of people think that's where Mary Shelley got the idea for *Frankenstein*. Doctors were searching for what they called the life force."

Nick rubbed his temples. This whole thing was giving him a headache. "So let me get this straight. You're thinking that Dr. Dippel believes all this garbage? That electricity can bring dead guys back to life?"

"It's not as crazy as it sounds," Dana said. "Every day people are discovering more and more about the connection between electricity and the human body. A jolt from a heart defibrillator can save someone having a heart attack. Electroconvulsive therapy is used on people with depression. Electrical currents control your eyes, your brain, and your heart."

"What if he did it?" Angie whispered. "What if Dippel figured out how to use electricity to bring dead people to life? What if that's why he's collecting bodies?"

A horrible thought occurred to Nick. "The football team," he said. "Maybe those kids were so big because they weren't kids at all. Maybe they were corpses he brought back to life. A team of monsters he was experimenting with."

"Jake." Tiffany gave a small squeal. "Are you saying Jake is a . . ."

"No," Carter said, his face red. "Jake is *not* a monster. He's my friend."

This was too much to take in at one time. Hundreds of thoughts flowed through Nick's mind. Dead bodies coming to life. Crazy experiments straight out of a horror movie. A mad scientist in a castle right in the middle of an otherwise normal California city. He never would have believed it if he hadn't seen some pretty strange things himself.

He scrubbed his hands through his hair. "Here's the one thing I still don't get. Let's say it's all true. Let's say Dippel really is stealing bodies and bringing them back to life. Why would he kidnap Cody? Cody's already alive. What use would he be in Dippel's tests?"

While the rest of them were talking, Dana had been slowly reading through her book. About three quarters of the way from the end, she put her hand to her mouth, "Oh, my gosh!"

"What's wrong?" Angie asked.

Dana shook her head, her eyes glassy and her face nearly as pale as the Sumina Prep headmaster's. "How could I not have known this? I've read *Frankenstein* three or four times." She wiped a palm across her damp forehead. "There was another scientist who experimented with bioelectricity at the same time. But he didn't just study science. He also studied philosophy and religion. He claimed to have invented something called the elixir of life.

Nick didn't get it. "What's so bad about that?"

Dana bit her lip. She looked like she was going to cry. "This scientist went further than any of the others. In his writings he talked about soul transference—sending

169

the soul of one person into the body of another. It's rumored that he actually tried it with a couple of corpses."

"Calm down," Nick said. "Just because some guy did crazy experiments two hundred years ago doesn't mean anyone would do something like that now."

"You don't understand," Dana said, physically shaking. "The scientist who did those experiments was born in the actual Castle Frankenstein."

Angelo sucked in his breath. "I thought the Sumina Prep building looked familiar. That's where I've seen it before. It looks just like the paintings of the original Castle Frankenstein, in Germany."

"There's more," Dana said. "The name of that scientist—the one who tried to move people's souls—was Johann Konrad . . . Dippel."

Angelo scratched his head and wrote nothing in his notebook. "Look," he said, turning the page around. "If you take Sumina, and reverse the letters, it's *animus*. That's Latin for 'life force.' They're going to try to steal Cody's animus. His soul."

Nick tried to convince himself that the idea of stealing somone's soul was crazy. But there were too many clues for them all to be coincidences. "We have to go back there," he said.

Carter shook his head violently back and forth. "We can't. Didn't you hear that crazy dude say he was going to make sure the school was locked up tight? Besides, he'd be expecting us. Next time none of us might make it out."

Nick's hands were trembling so bad he had to put them flat on the table. "You want to just leave him there while they suck out his soul?"

"For all we know, they've already done it," Tiffany said.

"I don't think so." Dana tapped the open page of the book. "All of these experiments have to do with electricity right? Doesn't anyone think it's sort of a big coincidence that the last time Dippel stole bodies was right before a big lightning storm?"

"You're right!" Angelo said. "That's got to be what all the wires are for. He must need to store a huge amount of electricity to do his tests. Remember all the electricity we saw in his lab?"

"And there hasn't been a lightning storm since then." Nick slammed his fist on the table, earning a dirty look from a woman reading a book about babies. "But tomorrow night there's supposed to be a huge storm. We have to go."

"Nick's right," Angie said. "We might still have a

chance to save Cody. But even if we can't, Dippel won't stop there. Maybe kids have more life source than grown-ups. Next time they could grab some innocent kid off the street. It could be your one of your brothers or sisters, Carter. We have to stop this."

Carter crumpled his candy-bar wrapper in his hand. "Okay, I'm in. What's the plan?"

"We can't do anything today," Dana said. "My parents are expecting the three of us to spend the night. We could link up by computer with you guys after dinner."

"Good idea," Nick said.

The six of them left the library. It was still raining, and even though it was only a little after six, the clouds were so thick it looked like night outside.

"You want to head back to my house?" Nick asked.

"Probably a good idea," Carter said. "My brothers and sisters would bug us anyway."

"I'll need to check with my parents," Nick said. "But it should be okay." He started to walk to his bike before remembering he needed to get a book about something other than monsters. As he turned back toward the library, a figure stepped out of the shadows. It was tall and broad shouldered. It was too dark to see the figure's face, but he was aiming something at the kids.

"Look out!" Nick called as the figure stepped toward them.

"I bringsies back hers toysies," a familiar voice said. He was holding a red-and-white rectangle; it took Nick a moment to recognize as Tiffany's cell phone.

Carter burst into a huge grin, ran forward, and wrapped his arms around the giant's waist. "Jake," he cried. "I thought you were out of the country."

173

CHAPTER 20

MOM, DAD, CAN I KEEP HIM?

"Look at you," Carter said, grasping one of the giant's huge hands in both of his. "I can't believe you're here."

Angelo took off his wet tortoiseshell glasses, wiped them on his sleeve, and shoved them back on his nose. "The question is, how did he get here?"

"Runsies on footsies," Jake said, bouncing up and down in a puddle. Dressed in a Sumina Prep sweatshirt as big as a pup tent and a huge pair of gray sweatpants, he seemed to be as excited about finding the kids as Carter was to have him there.

Jake held the cell phone toward Tiffany. She licked her lips before stretching out one hand to take it. "Um, thanks."

"That's all you have to say?" Carter growled. "He runsies twenty miles on his footsies to bring you your phone and you say, 'Um, thanks'?"

Jake patted the top of his own head. "Pret-ty hair-sies."

Tiffany forced a smile, clearly a little freaked out now that she knew what Jake was. "Yes, your hair is very pretty."

"Not to be a party pooper or anything," Angie said, rain dripping down her face, "but is anyone else wondering how he found us? And if the mad scientist is somewhere nearby too?"

Nick looked around, wondering if a bunch of Sumina Prep creatures were going to grab them.

"Maybe he got my address off my phone?" Tiffany suggested.

"I'm not sure he knows how to use a cell phone," Dana said. "And even if does, he would go to your house, not the library."

Jake gave a deep sniff, flaring his broad nostrils, pointed at Tiffany, and clapped. "Is to be follows flowersies."

"He smelled you," Carter crowed. "I said you wore too much perfume."

Tiffany sneered.

Angelo scratched his head. "He followed her scent from twenty miles away? I think Dr. Dippel is doing more than bringing dead bodies back to life. A sense of smell that strong is like some kind of superpower."

At the sound of the headmaster's name, Jake ducked his head and shuddered.

"He's scared," Carter said, patting Jake's hand. "It's okay. We won't let that psycho freak hurt you."

"What do we do with him?" Nick asked. "Pretty sure I'm not going to be able to convince my parents this is the new kid in class."

Jake pointed at Tiffany, a huge grin spreading across his face. "His going with flowersies."

"No way," Tiffany said at once. "He's not coming with me."

"I guess we could take him to *my* house," Angelo said, rubbing the side of his nose. "Hopefully, my mom will spend most of the evening working in her greenhouse."

"Okay then," Angie said. "You four go to Angelo's and we'll go to Dana's. Let's plan on meeting online at eight."

Nick, Jake, and Angelo set off through the rain, taking all the side streets they could, to avoid being seen. In the dark and rain, Nick hoped no one would notice

176

them, anyway. But at seven feet tall, it wasn't like Jake fit in. He expected they would need to ride their bikes slowly for the giant to keep up, but it turned out Jake could run as fast as they could peddle without even breathing hard.

Halfway home, Jake's stomach began to growl.

"Let's take him to McDonald's," Carter said. "I'll bet he could eat, like, twenty Big Macs."

"Macksies," Jake repeated happily.

"Oh, yeah. That wouldn't draw any attention," Nick said. The wind was gusting so hard, he had to lean into it to keep from being blown over. The raindrops stung his face. "Do you have anything at your house to eat?" he asked Angelo.

"I think we have a couple of frozen pizzas," Angelo called back.

By the time they reached Angelo's house, Jake was looking worn down. His eyes seemed glassy, and he stumbled going up the steps.

"What's wrong with him?" Carter asked.

Angelo shook his head. "I'm not sure. Let's get him into my room where I can get a better look at him."

Jake ducked his head to avoid a hanging lamp and followed the boys down the hallway. When Angelo opened his door, the giant squeezed his bulk through and looked happily around. Jake collapsed onto Angelo's bed. The frame groaned so loudly Nick was sure it was going to break. Somehow the bed managed to hold Jake's weight, although it was definitely sagging in the middle.

"He's probably hungry," Carter said. "I know I am." He patted Jake on the shoulder. "Do you want some pizza?"

"Piz-zies," Jake mumbled. His voice sounded slow and thick, like a windup toy running down. The giant pulled up the front of his shirt, and Nick noticed something set into his stomach where his belly button should have been.

"Hey," Nick said, kneeling down for a closer view. "What is this?" Two flat metal prongs and one round one stuck about an inch out of Jake's skin.

Angelo leaned over his shoulder. "Of course." He rummaged under his bed and pulled out an orange extension cable. "Quick, plug this into the wall."

"What are you doing?" Carter shouted as Angelo connected the female end of the extension cord to the prong sticking out of Jake's stomach. "You're going to electrocute him."

"No," Angelo said. "Watch."

As soon as Nick plugged in the cord, Jake's eyes

178

began to return to normal. "Go-ood."

Nick glanced at the cord plugged into the wall on one end and into Jake on the other. This was so totally bizarre. "Is he some kind of robot?"

"Not at all." Angelo patted the giant, who was looking better and better by the minute. "It's just that whatever force Dippel used to bring him to life must run down over time. He must need a recharge every so often."

"Cool!" Carter said. "I wish I could recharge myself."

"Can you keep an eye on him while we go home and get our stuff?" Nick asked.

Angelo looked at Jake, who was petting the pillow and murmuring, "Soffffft."

"Sure," he said, not sounding sure at all.

Nick biked home as quickly as he could, packed clothes, pajamas, and toiletries, and explained to his parents that he, Carter, and Angelo were going to spend the night.

"Please tell me you're not watching another monster marathon," his mom said.

Nick grimaced. "Not if I can help it."

"Where's your book?" Dad asked just as Nick was trying to slip out the back door.

Nick hesitated. "Um, I found a great nonfiction book

179

on scientists of the seventeen hundreds. It was really cool. But it was a reference book, so they wouldn't let me check it out."

"Scientists of the seventeen hundreds?" Mom asked, clearly skeptical.

"Yeah, this one guy, uh, Luigi Galvani, was a pioneer in neuroelectrophysiology."

Dad nodded, clearly impressed. "I always wanted a neuroelectrophysiologist in the family. Either that or a proctologist."

"What's a proctologist?" Nick asked.

Mom rolled her eyes. "Never mind."

As Nick closed the back door, he heard his mom saying, "What kind of thing is that to say to your son?"

When Nick got to Angelo's house, Angelo met him at the front door. "How's he holding up?" Nick asked.

Angelo shook his head. "*He's* holding up fine. *I'm* a nervous wreck."

Nick sniffed. "Smells like pizza."

"After Jake finished recharging, I cooked two extra-large," Angelo said. "One for me and one for him. Before I could ask him if he wanted pepperoni or sausage, he ate both of them. He rolled them up together like a giant burrito and downed them in three bites. The hot cheese didn't seem to bother him at all."

"I guess they don't have pizza where he comes from?" Nick said.

"Not for long if he's around." They walked down the hallway to Angelo's room. "Since then he's eaten six Ding Dongs, three cans of SpaghettiOs, a full box of Lucky Charms, and all of our leftover turkey. I never thought I'd say this, but I think I'd rather have Carter over for dinner."

"I heard that," Carter called from the bedroom.

A moment after Nick and Angelo walked in, a sulfur-like stench hit them. "Dude," Nick said, waving his hand in front of his face. "That's nasty."

"Don't blame me," Carter said, tilting his head in Jake's direction.

Jake grabbed a pillow and pressed it to his face, pointing at Carter. Apparently he was sensitive to more smells than Tiffany's perfume.

"Tattletale," Carter muttered.

"It's almost eight," Angelo said. He sat down at his computer, adjusted the webcam on top of his monitor to take in most of the room, and booted up a screen-sharing program while Nick opened and closed the bedroom door trying to clear away some of the stink.

A few seconds later Dana appeared on the monitor. "Hi, guys," she said, peering into her screen. "Hey, nice sentinel."

"Thanks," Angelo said, glancing over at the movie replica on his desk. The silver sphere with twin blades sticking out was the weapon of choice of the Tall Man in the Phantasm movies.

Dana adjusted her webcam until she, Angie, and Tiffany came into view. Angie was studying some kind of map while Tiffany polished her toenails.

"How's he doing?" Dana asked.

Angelo checked on Jake. Now that the smell had cleared from the room, he was lying on the bed, licking spaghetti sauce off his fingers. "Well, he likes comic books. X-Men seems to be his favorite so far."

Angie looked up from her map. "What's our first plan of action?"

Nick moved a chair next to Angelo. "The thing I can't figure out is where Dippel is hiding Cody. He took us through the whole school."

Jake moaned softly and buried his face in his comic book.

"I don't think he likes it when we mention you-know-who's name," Carter said.

"I might have a clue." Angelo clicked a button on

the computer and the screen split into two images. One half still showed Angie, Dana, and Tiffany. The other half showed a run-down castle that appeared to be more ruins than walls. "This is Castle Frankenstein as it looks now in Germany."

"Wait." Nick looked at the image on the monitor. "If the castle's still in Germany, how can it be here?"

"That doesn't look anything like the school," Angie said, seeing the same image on Dana's monitor.

"I was confused by that at first too," Angelo said. "Until I found this." He clicked his mouse and the image changed to an old black-and-white sketch. "This is what Castle Frankenstein looked like when it was built in the twelve hundreds."

Dana's eyes opened wide. "It's a perfect match."

"It looks that way," Angelo agreed. "It was later divided into two parts, and eventually enlarged. But sometime in the eighteenth century it fell into ruins. My guess is that either Dr. Dippel was lying when he said his castle was assembled from the original stones, or possibly sometime between when it was built and fell into ruins, the family moved the original castle and replaced it with another one."

"Great research," Nick said, "but that still doesn't answer my question."

Angelo held up a finger. "Patience. Patience. This was trickier to find." He moved to another picture that it took Nick a minute to figure out.

"Blueprints," Dana said.

"They didn't call them blueprints back then," Angelo said. "But from everything I can find, these appear to be the most accurate plans of the original castle's layout. My guess is these are what Dippel used to build his version." He clicked through a series of pictures showing the first floor, the second floor, the third floor, and the towers.

"It looks just like what he showed us on the tour," Carter said, searching the bottom of the Lucky Charms box for any colored marshmallow shapes Jake might have missed.

"That's what I thought too," Angelo said. "But then I found . . ." He clicked to a final set of plans for rooms Nick didn't remember from their tour.

"What is that?" he asked.

Angelo grinned. "A lower level Dippel never told us about."

CHAPTER 21
I LOVE IT WHEN A PLAN COMES TOGETHER

"That has to be it," Angie said. "Dippel must be hiding Cody there. Does it show how to get down there?"

Angelo moved his mouse to a set of circular stairs that descended from a center room. "This is how you went down back then. But obviously Dippel has changed the plans. I don't remember seeing a staircase anywhere."

"Maybe Jake can help us," Nick said. He turned to the giant. "Do you know how to get to the lower level of the school?"

Jake dropped his comic book and put his hands over his face, swaying back and forth.

"I don't think he's going to be much help," Carter

said. He patted Jake's shoulder and gave him back his comic book. "Look at this page. That's Emma Frost. She's totally hot."

"Great," Nick said. "So we have to break into a locked school, locate a hidden entrance, and avoid Dr. Di—I mean, you know who."

"It might be worse than that," Tiffany said, fanning her toenails to help the polish dry. "Has anyone considered that since Jake is still here, maybe the rest of the students are too? They weren't exactly friendly the last time we were there."

Nick groaned. This was beginning to sound impossible.

"There might be a way," Dana said. "Give me control of the screen."

Angelo raised his eyebrows and changed a setting on the screen-share program so the half without the picture showed Dana's computer screen. She typed in the web address for the city of Diablo Valley and clicked on a link that said *Official City Use Only*.

"You have to have a password to access that," Angelo said.

Tiffany sniffed, put down her polish, and inserted a thumb drive in the computer's USB port. She typed in a series of commands, waited, typed in a few more, and suddenly she was in the locked section of the site.

"How did you do that?" Angelo asked as Tiffany returned to her toenails.

Angie chuckled. "Maybe you don't know as much about us as you think."

Tiffany was a computer hacker? Nick would never have guessed that in a million years.

"Let's see now." Dana explored the website until she found what she was looking for. "Streets and sewers," she murmured. Engineering plans whizzed by. "Here we go," she said, stopping on the section of the map where Sumina Prep was located.

Nick studied the streets. "I don't see the school."

"That's because these are plans from ten years ago," Angelo said.

"Right." Dana moved the mouse. "There used to be a factory where the castle is now. I read an article about it getting shut down in the paper. A lot of people lost their jobs, and some questions were raised about why Dippel was moving his school from Transnistria to California in the first place. It seems Transnistrian officials were looking into his experiments right before he left."

"Then why did they let him open the school?" Carter asked.

"Dippel paid off enough officials that they stopped complaining. And, he promised a winning football program. It was the perfect combination. He could test his minions in public without anyone asking questions, and the city got their first winning sports team." She traced a thin gray line. "This is an old maintenance tunnel. It looks like it's still there, but I can't tell if it goes all the way to the school."

"I don't know," Angelo said. "For all we know, the tunnel's been filled in since this, or it dead ends."

Dana printed a copy of the plans and closed the city website. "It's still our best shot. Unless you'd rather face you know who and his army of you know whats."

Carter groaned. "Some fall break this is turning out to be."

"Fallsies breaksies being turning," Jake agreed.

• • •

The next morning, Nick woke up with a stiff neck from sleeping on the floor in Angelo's room. "What'cha doing?" he asked Angelo, who was leafing through a thick electronics catalog.

"Making a parts list," Angelo said. "Once we get into the school, we still have to figure out a way to stop Dippel."

Angelo's closet door swung open and Carter stumbled out, rubbing his eyes.

"Did you sleep in there?" Nick asked.

Carter groaned. "Tried to. Jake snored so loud I'm surprised he didn't collapse the roof. Even closing the closet door didn't help."

"I didn't hear anything," Nick said.

"That's because you were asleep." Carter groaned and stretched.

Nick glanced around, suddenly realizing Jake wasn't in the room. "Where is he?" he yelped, panicked at the idea of the giant wandering around the neighborhood.

Angelo pointed down the hallway, still studying his catalog. "My mom went in to the office this morning, so I let him watch TV. He's a big fan of Dora the Explorer."

"You can't let him watch that stuff," Carter growled. "It'll rot his brain."

The three boys walked down the hall to find Jake sitting in the living room, eyes glued to the TV. Surrounding him on the floor were three cereal boxes, a bread wrapper minus the bread, and an empty jug of orange juice.

"I see he's still got his appetite," Nick said, kicking a cereal box. There wasn't a single crumb left at the bottom.

189

Angelo shook his head. "All I have to say is I'm not going to be the one who shows him how to use a flush toilet when this stuff works its way through his digestive tract."

A few minutes later, as the boys were making their own breakfast from what little Jake hadn't devoured, the doorbell rang. Angelo went to the door and let Angie, Dana, and Tiffany in.

As soon as Tiffany walked into the house, Jake jumped to his feet. The giant sniffed. "No flowersies?"

Tiffany blushed. "No. No perfume today."

"Nice call," Carter whispered to Jake.

"Okay," Angie said, pulling a handful of papers out of her backpack. "I've been putting together a plan."

"Who put you in charge?" Nick asked.

"Do *you* have a plan?"

Nick scratched the back of his neck. He turned to Angelo, hoping he had put something together, but his friend appeared deeply engrossed in his catalog. Carter, despite his earlier complaints, was sitting beside Jake, eating cereal and watching Swiper the fox try to steal Dora's lunch.

"Right then," Angie said. "Back to the plan. The first thing we need to do is get in and out of the castle. I'm taking that part. Once we get there, we have to figure out how to stop Dippel."

Angelo raised his hand as though they were all in a classroom and Angie was the teacher. "I'm working on it."

"Perfect," Angie said, checking off a box. Nick couldn't stand the way she was bossing everyone around, but since he hadn't thought to come up with a plan of his own, he had to let her continue. She also seemed to be enjoying this way too much, like it was some kind of school science project instead of a matter of life and death. "Next on the list are weapons."

"You mean like guns?" Nick asked. The idea of blazing into Dippel's castle with machine guns and rocket launchers was way cool. If Angie could get her hands on some serious artillery, he wouldn't mind her being in charge at all.

"Do you *have* any guns?" Angie asked.

"Not really," Nick admitted, pretty sure paintball and airsoft didn't count.

"Then we need to come up with some weapons of our own. Who can I put down for that?" Angie held her pen poised above the paper, waiting for volunteers.

"I've got some ideas," Dana said.

Angie nodded and made another check.

"I'll do some too," Carter called, still watching the television.

"You're going to make weapons?" Nick asked. "*Real* weapons. Not like Nerf swords and stuff."

Carter snorted. "Leave it to me. I'm the master of arcane and ancient armament."

"Good enough," Angie said. "The last problem is, how we are going to get big boy to the castle without being spotted?"

"He can run beside our bikes," Nick said. "He's heck'a fast."

Angie shook her head. "Have you looked outside? It's stopped raining for a while. But it doesn't look like it's done. Besides, it's freezing out. I'm not riding my bike all the way to Diablo Valley."

Tiffany tapped her lips with one finger. "Hmm," she murmured. "I might have an idea."

"I'll put you down for it," Angie said. She turned to Nick. "What are you going to do?"

"Don't worry about me." Nick sneered and tapped the side of his head. "I'm hard at work in here."

Angie rolled her eyes and scribbled on her paper. "I'll list you as doing nothing."

CHAPTER 22

JAMES BOND HAS NOTHING ON THESE KIDS

The truth was that Nick really didn't know what he was going to do. When it was him, Angelo, and Carter, Nick had usually been the one in charge, making decisions and coming up with ideas. As he walked back to his house, he tried to think of some way he could help. But all he could think about was how Angie had taken over everything. Even his own friends were treating her like the new leader. He wished it was just the Three Monsterteers again, even if Angie and her friends did have some pretty good ideas.

"How was the sleepover?" Dad asked when Nick walked through the door. He was still working on his wrecked plane.

"Okay, I guess." Nick washed a green apple and took a bite.

"Where are the guys?" Dad ripped a long piece of duct tape off the roll and wrapped it repeatedly around one wing.

Nick sighed. "Letting Angie Hollingsworth boss them around."

"Ahhh, girl trouble." Dad set down his plane and crossed his legs. "Well that's one area where I can definitely help you. What would you like to know about? How to get a girl to like you? What it means when she punches you over and over on the shoulder until you get a really nasty bruise and have to go to the school nurse? Or do you want to know about smooching? There's a reason I was known as Luscious Lips Braithwaite back in the day."

"I heard it was Liver Lips," Mom called from the other room.

"No, it's nothing like that," Nick said. "I just want things the way they used to be."

Dad tilted his head, looking critically at the plane that Nick suspected would never fly again. "Things change, Nick. That's the way life is. You can either spend all your time wishing for the way things were or

194

adjusting to how they are. But I can tell you this much: People who spend all their time wishing for the past don't accomplish much in the future." He winked at Nick and whispered, "Your mom almost never punches me in the arm anymore. And she called me Luscious Lips just last night."

"Gross," Nick said. He took his apple up to his room and thought about what his dad had said. Not the kissing part, which was just nasty. But about recognizing that things changed. Maybe he was right. Maybe he needed to live with the fact that it was never going to be just the three of them again. The thought made him a little sad.

The rest of the day he tried to think of anything that might help with the plan. For a while he tried dreaming up useful inventions. But inventing was really Angelo's thing. He thought about trying to find a way to make flaming paintballs. But he was pretty sure paintball guns weren't allowed on the BART trains anyway.

Eventually he turned on the TV and watched a Harry Potter movie marathon until it was time to meet his friends.

At eight he headed out the door. "I'm going to hang out with Carter and Angelo," he called.

"And Angie?" Dad asked, wiggling his eyebrows.

Nick snorted.

"Be safe," Mom said. "The weather is supposed to get pretty bad tonight. They're saying there's supposed to be lightning storms tonight, and maybe even snow."

Nick was surprised. Snow in the mountains was common in California, but they almost never got it where he lived. The idea of facing Dr. Dippel and his minions in a fierce winter storm was almost too much to deal with. For a moment, he considered giving the whole thing up.

Instead, he headed out the door. Angie might be bossy, and Angelo and Carter might be annoying at times. But he'd promised them he would be there and he wasn't about to let them down.

They met in front of Angie's house at 8:30. Dana was standing beside a large canvas bag and Angelo was messing with another of his gizmos when Nick pulled up. "Where's Carter?" Angie demanded, bossy as ever.

"No idea," Nick said. "Where's Jake?"

Angie pointed toward the house. Angelo tweaked something on his gizmo and it gave a shrill wail of feedback before he turned it down.

"What's that supposed to be?" Nick asked.

196

Angelo turned off a switch on the side of the box and wrapped a pair of black and red cables with alligator clips on their ends around it. "I call it my polarity-reversing overload generator. PROG. If we get close enough to whatever Dippel is doing, I should be able to blow out all of his electrical circuits with this."

A couple of big wet raindrops hit Nick on the top of his head. "My mom said it could snow tonight."

"That will make even better cover," Angie said. If she was nervous, she didn't show it.

A bike came speeding down the street. "Sorry I'm late!" Carter yelled.

"Keep it down," Angie whispered. "My mom's at work. But I don't want any of the neighbors telling her I had boys over."

Nick eyed the white case Carter had hung over his shoulder. "Is that a pillow?"

Carter bit the inside of his cheek. "Sort of." He pulled out his feather pillow, his face turning red.

Angie frowned. "Please tell me that's not your idea of a weapon. Somehow I don't think animated corpses are going to be scared off by a good pillow fight."

"Unless you're planning on singing them to sleep," Dana said with a sly grin.

197

"Very funny." Carter fished around in the pillow-case. "My weapons are inside." He pulled out a handful of white packets.

Nick groaned. "Itching powder? You brought itching powder?"

"That's not all." Carter reached into the pillowcase again and removed a glass of blue liquid.

Angie giggled. "Your weapons are itching powder and *aftershave*."

"What?" Carter turned the bottle around. "Oh, I thought it was rubbing alcohol. You know, to throw in their eyes or light on fire."

Nick felt like pulling his hair out. He grabbed the pillowcase and looked inside. Other than the itching powder and aftershave, the only things in the case were a down pillow and a bunch of chocolaty granola bars. He glared at Carter.

"Okay, fine." Carter sighed. "I was tired because I didn't get any sleep last night. I was just going to take a short nap. But when I woke up it was eight. So I grabbed my pillow and threw in anything I could find."

Carter was a good friend, and as loyal as could be. But sometimes he was absolutely maddening. "Tell me you did better," Nick said to Dana.

Dana emptied her bag on the ground, and at first Nick thought it was going to be Carter all over again. Lying on the grass at her feet were three fishing poles, a pair of baseball bats, and what looked like soda cans wrapped in duct tape.

Carter laughed. "So I'm going to put my monsters to sleep while you take yours fishing."

Dana picked up one of the poles. Two hooks hung from the end of a pair of silvery strings. She pointed the fishing rod toward a lamppost. But instead of casting, she pushed a button on the side of the reel. A powerful spring launched the silver lines. The hooks hit the post and tangled around it. Dana pushed another button and an electrical arc raced from one hook to another. Overhead, the light exploded, sending showers of blue sparks to the street below.

"Whoa!" Carter gulped. "That beats my itching powder."

"Over fifty thousand volts of electricity," Dana said.

"It's a homemade Taser," Angelo murmured, clearly in awe.

Nick rubbed his hands together nervously. "Would it kill someone?"

Dana walked to the lamppost, untangled the hooks,

and reeled in the line. "No, but it will temporarily disrupt their sensory and motor-control nerves. One shot from this and they'll be out of commission for a good ten to fifteen minutes."

Angie nodded, pleased. "And the bats?"

"Just over seven hundred thousand volts. More like a stun gun. Each of the poles is good for five stuns. The bats will run out of juice after two or three."

Nick whistled. This was some serious hardware. He pointed at the cans. "I take it those aren't Diet Cokes then, huh?"

Dana hefted one of the tape-wrapped cylinders. There were six of them. "Classic smoke grenades. Pull the tab, count to three, and throw. Two yellow, two white, and two purple."

Angelo shook his head. "I'm impressed."

Carter dropped the itching powder and aftershave back into his pillowcase. "Anybody want a granola bar?"

Tiffany snorted.

"Now all we need is Jake," Angie said. "Tiffany's working on a way to get him onto the train without freaking people out."

Nick glanced around the yard. "If she got him camouflaged, she did an amazing job."

"Ha ha," Angie said sarcastically. "You should be a comedian." She walked to the door and knocked. "You ready in there?"

The door swung partway open and Tiffany stepped onto the porch. "Before I bring Jake out," she said, "I want to remind you all that he's sort of sensitive about his looks. So don't make fun of him."

"Why would we make—" Nick started to ask when Tiffany opened the door the rest of the way and Jake stepped through.

Nick's mouth hung open. He blinked, unable to believe what he was seeing. Tiffany had dressed the giant in red, white, and blue stripes. His face was covered with white makeup, except for the blue triangles around his eyes and the red on his lips. His nose was covered by a bright red ball and his hair was tucked under a rainbow-colored wig.

"A clown?" Carter gasped in horror. "You turned Jake into a clown? How could you?"

Jake shifted from one foot to the other, seeming uncomfortable with all the attention he was getting.

Nick tried to catch his breath. He'd never seen anything like it before. "Okay, I give up. How are we supposed to sneak a seven-foot clown onto the train?"

"You aren't," Tiffany said. "That's exactly the point.

I kept trying to think of a way to hide a seven-foot giant. Until I finally realized you can't. He's huge. There's no way people aren't going to notice him. That's when I knew I had to go the other direction. People see a bunch of kids with a seven-foot man, they start to ask questions. They see a bunch of kids with a seven-foot clown, they think they must be coming back from a circus. It's called hiding in plain sight."

Nick couldn't help grinning. It was either the stupidest idea ever or pure genius.

CHAPTER 23

THIS CHAPTER GIVES ME A HEADACHE

"Mommy, Mommy, look. A clown!" Half a dozen little kids stood around Jake, staring in delight at the giant in the bright red nose as the train raced toward Diablo Valley.

"Does he juggle?" a five-year-old girl asked.

"Does he breathe fire?"

A little boy held out his hand and said, "Give me five, Mr. Clown."

Nick leaned forward, afraid Jake would slap the kid's hand right off. But the giant brushed his fingers gently across the boy's palm and slapped each of the other kids five before Tiffany said, "Time to give Mr. Clown a rest. He's tired from doing lots of shows."

Nick glanced at Carter, who was slouched in his seat listening to his MP3 player, and tugged on his coat sleeve. "What's with the music?"

Carter pulled out an earbud. "It calms me down. If it wasn't for the music, I think I'd be totally freaking out right now."

Nick knew the feeling. He leaned over to Angelo, who was still adjusting his polarity-reversing overload generator. "You think that thing will really work?"

Angelo wet his lips. "I'd give it about a seventy-seven percent probability of success."

Nick didn't like the sound of that. They could get all the way to their goal and still have a twenty-three percent chance of failure. Sooner than he would have liked, the train shuddered to a stop at their station. Angie was the first one off. At least he had to give her credit for being brave.

Outside, the rain had changed to fat white flakes that drifted down so thick it was hard to see more than ten feet in any direction. The few other people at the station stuck out their tongues and hands, laughing as they tried to catch flakes.

Jake looked up at the swirling crystals, eyes wide with wonder. "Rainsies are to being coldsies. Pret-ty."

"Yes, the snow is pretty," said Tiffany, tugging him

by the arm and leading him down the platform steps.

Angie examined her maps, which she'd had the foresight to cover with plastic sleeves. "The tunnel entrance should be about halfway up the hill on the west side of the road—if it's still there. If it's not, this plan could come to a quick end."

"What'd she say?" Carter asked, removing an earbud.

Nick could hear a faint tune that sounded vaguely familiar. "She said, 'Turn off your music and pay attention.' "

Carter grimaced but turned off his player.

Once they were away from the station, they could see no one else but themselves. No people, no cars. It was like they were exploring a frigid wilderness. Angie took turns checking the GPS on Tiffany's phone and comparing it to her map.

"There," Angelo said, pointing to a concrete bunker built into the side of the hill. With the falling snow, the light-colored concrete was easy to miss. Nick was impressed Angelo had spotted it at all.

They were about to cross the road when Nick saw movement from the corner of his eye. "Wait. Stop," he hissed.

Angie glanced back at him over her shoulder. "What is it?"

"Not sure," Nick said. Then he saw it again. This time he knew exactly what it was and his heart pounded against his ribs. "Get down. Get down," he whispered.

The six of them dropped to the snow-covered asphalt. Jake saw what they were doing and fell down too, grinning like it was a game. A moment later, two hulking shapes appeared, walking side by side.

"The football players," Carter whispered, his voice shaking. "What are they doing out here?"

"Nothing good," Nick said.

Jake saw his fellow students and pointed—a big grin spreading across his face. He started to call out to them, but Tiffany slapped a hand over his mouth and put a finger to her lips. "Shhh. Hidesies."

The giant's eyes glowed. Tiffany was speaking his language. "Hidesies," he whispered back, putting a finger to his own lips.

As soon as the football players disappeared from view, Angie got up. "Okay, let's cross."

"Hang on," Nick said. He wasn't sure why, but he had a feeling they should wait.

Angie gave him an irritated glare, but she dropped back to the ground. Less than five minutes later, two more Sumina Prep players marched into view. One of them walked to the concrete bunker and tested the metal door before moving on.

"Patrols," Dana growled. "Dippel's expecting us."

Angelo chewed at the tip of his thumbnail. "Either that or he's just increased security in general."

"Let's time them and see how often they come by," Angie said.

They crept back to the minimal cover of dead grass on the other side of the road and watched for the next twenty minutes. "Four and half minutes, almost like clockwork," Angie said when the pair had passed for the fifth time.

Nick's nose felt like an icicle and his legs were going numb. He rubbed his gloved hands across his face, trying to warm up his cheeks. "If we're going to do something, we better do it soon. I'm freezing."

Angie checked with Dana. "What do you think?"

Dana reached into her bag and pulled out a smoke grenade and two fishing poles. She handed one of the poles to Angie and kept the other. Nick gritted his teeth. Didn't she think he could handle a weapon?

Dana handed him the grenade. "At four minutes, pull the grenade and throw it in the middle of the road. If we're lucky, Dippel's minions will think it's part of the storm. We'll run to the door, and when we signal, get across the road fast. We're only going to have a few

207

minutes to get the door open and get inside the tunnel."

Angie checked her watch, counting down when it had nearly been four minutes. "Three, two, one, *now*."

Nick pulled the metal tab on the can. There was a small click. "Count to three and throw it," Dana reminded.

"I know," Nick snapped. He rolled the can under-handed onto the road so it made as little noise as possible. The grenade came to a stop almost exactly in the center. A second later, there was a thump and an impressive cloud of white smoke filled the air.

"Let's go," Dana said. Together, she and Angie disappeared into the smoke.

"What do we do if they don't signal?" Carter asked, squeezing his MP3 player to his chest.

"Leave Tiffany here with Jake and run," Nick joked.

Tiffany scowled.

Just when Nick was beginning to wonder if Dana's plan had gone wrong, two blue flashes of light illuminated the smoke cloud, one right on top of the other, followed by a pair of thumps.

A soft whistle sounded. *Tweet-tweet. Tweet-tweet.*

"Let's go," Nick said. The five of them jumped to their feet and ran across the road.

"Hidesies," Jake whispered gleefully.

On the other side of the road, Angie and Dana were untangling their fishing hooks from a pair of uncon- scious bodies nearly as big as Jake. They were both wearing the Sumina Prep sweatshirts and sweatpants Jake had arrived in.

Jake leaned across his fellow students and shook them gently, eyes worried. "Sleepsies?"

"Let's let them sleep," Tiffany said.

"What happens when they recover?" Carter asked.

Dana's lips pulled up in a worried half smile. "If we're lucky, they won't know what hit them. If we aren't . . . then we better hope the tunnel leads to the school."

Nick ran to the metal door and tried to turn the knob. His heart sank. "It's locked," he said. Of course it was locked. Who would leave an access tunnel open for anyone to explore? Why hadn't they considered that?

"Maybe Jake can knock it down?" Tiffany said.

Angie shook her head. "That metal looks thick. And besides, even if he could, the sound would carry all the way to the school."

"Let me have a look," Carter said. He walked up to the door and leaned over to study the lock. A moment later he reached into his jacket and pulled out his pock- etknife, tweezers, and a paper clip. He slipped the knife into the crack between the door and jamb, bent the

209

paper clip, and poked it into the lock.

"If this is anything like your weapons," Angie said, "we really don't have—"

Carter grabbed the paper clip with the tweezers, pulled, and there was an audible click. A moment later the door swung open.

"Dude," Nick said. "How'd you learn to do that?"

"Cub Scouts," Carter said, putting his tools back in his coat. "Our den leader was a locksmith."

"And he taught you to pick locks?" Tiffany asked.

Carter grinned. "It beat building birdhouses."

As they stepped through the door, a set of motion-activated lights turned on, illuminating the dusty tunnel.

As Carter helped Jake out of his costume, Nick thought things might not be so bad after all. But they'd barely gone a hundred feet into the tunnel when a deafening scream filled the concrete passage. Nick slapped his hands to his ears, but it didn't help at all. The noise was like a high-pitched drill cutting directly into his head.

"What is it?" he shouted, barely able to hear his voice over the wailing. It was like the noise wasn't even coming through his ears at all, but being broadcast directly into his head.

Angie searched the tunnel, her teeth clenched in pain, before pointing to something on the ceiling. "There." Her mouth moved, but Nick could only make out what she was saying by reading her lips.

Nick looked up and saw a jar just like the one that had been at the front of the first classroom in the school. Floating in the middle of it was a quivering human brain. He didn't know how, but he was almost positive the sound was coming from the jar. It hurt so bad, his eyes were watering. If it didn't stop soon, he was sure his head was going to split.

Dana pulled a baseball bat out of her bag.

"Shock it!" Nick screamed.

Angie shook her head and pointed to the bottle. Of course. Nick had forgotten that glass wasn't a conductor of electricity. Instead, Dana pulled back the bat. Before she could swing it, Jake caught her arm. Nick couldn't tell what the giant was shouting, but it was clear he didn't want Dana to smash the brain.

Was it because it was alive somehow? Is that what Jake was saying? Was the brain his friend too? Nick squeezed his hands against his ears. He couldn't take it much longer. "Do something!" he screamed.

Suddenly Tiffany reached into Carter's jacket and pulled out his MP3 player. She jumped toward Jake,

211

who swooped down to catch her in his arms. "Up," she yelled, pointing toward the jar. Jake lifted her until her face was almost level with the brain. Tiffany pushed a button on the music player, and pressed the earbuds against the jar.

A moment later the screaming cut off as abruptly as it had started. To Nick it felt like someone had just pulled an icepick out of his forehead. He gave a sigh of relief, his head still ringing.

"Good call," Angelo said. "How did you know that music would quiet it?"

Tiffany shrugged. "It calmed Carter down, and his brain isn't nearly this big."

"Very funny," Carter said. But even he seemed too relieved to stay mad for long.

Still pressing the headphones to the glass, Tiffany said, "Unless you want me to stay up here all night, I need something to attach these to the jar."

Dana reached into her bag and peeled some of the tape from one of her grenades. Struggling to keep the earbuds against the glass, Tiffany taped each of them to the jar, then taped the MP3 player itself so the whole thing stayed put.

"I bought that with my own money," Carter grumbled, staring up at his player.

"I'll get you another one if we make it out of this alive," Angelo said.

"You think there are any more of them?" Angie asked, searching the ceiling as they walked deeper into the tunnel.

"I hope not," Nick said. "That was our only set of tunes."

Dana put her bat back in her bag. "Do you think it was some kind of alarm?"

"Maybe," Angelo said. "Or it could just be a deterrent to keep people out."

"It definitely deterred me," Carter said.

Nick eased up next to Carter. "What was that song? It sounded sort of like Justin Bieber."

"Totally not," Carter said, his face going red.

Angelo snickered.

Ten minutes later they came around a corner and everyone stopped. A smooth concrete wall that looked much newer than the rest of the tunnel stretched from one side to the other.

Angie put her fingers against the wall, then slammed it with the palm of her hand before dropping to the floor. "It's a dead end!"

CHAPTER 24

PLUG YOUR NOSE FOR THIS PART

Nick sat next to Angie. "Maybe we can try the front door. Or find a way through the fence."

Angie shook her head, her hands in her lap. "No. By now they know someone attacked their patrol. We'd never make it within a hundred yards of the school. We'll be lucky if we can get back out."

"We tried," Dana said. "That should count for something."

Angie slammed her fist to the dusty floor. "Trying doesn't save Cody. Or the next kid Dippel grabs."

Nick knew exactly how she felt. Failure was failure and this one tasted terrible. Angelo sniffed and glanced at Carter. "Do you smell something bad?"

"Don't look at me," Carter said. "I haven't farted since we were on the train."

"Gross," Tiffany said. "I was sitting beside you."

Dana scrunched up her nose. "I *do* smell something."

Still covering his face with one hand, Jake pointed toward Carter. All eyes turned in his direction.

"Whaaat?" Carter said. "I swear it wasn't me."

Nick got up. "Move out of the way." He brushed cobwebs away from the wall where Carter had been standing. The concrete was old and crumbling, with a thin slime of green mold growing out of the cracks. "Give me your pocketknife," he said.

Carter handed Nick his knife. Nick opened the largest blade and began digging at the wall. The concrete flaked away easily, breaking off in bigger and bigger chunks the more he dug.

"I think there's something back there," Angelo said. Together, he and Nick dug away the last of the concrete, revealing a round metal plate.

"What is it?" Dana asked, joining them.

Angie came over. "See if you can pry it off."

The plate was covered with the same green mold as the wall, and the foul smell was even stronger. Nick slid the knife blade into the edge of the plate, working it back and forth.

"It's moving," Dana said.

Nick got his fingers onto the edge of the plate and pulled.

"Look out," Angelo cried.

The three of them jumped backward as the plate tilted out and then slammed to the ground, ringing like an old church bell. A horrible stench flowed out from the hole and they all covered their faces.

"Disgusting," Tiffany said.

Carter plugged his nose. "It smells worse than my little brother, and he *never* takes a bath," he said in a nasal voice.

Only Angie seemed unaffected by the stench. "Look at the water."

Nick glanced into the pipe. At the bottom a stream of goopy green liquid flowed slowly by. "So?"

"So this is how we get into the school." She grabbed a flashlight from her pack and shined it into the hole.

"You want to go *in* there?" Nick asked, his stomach rolling over. "I want to help Cody. But how do we know this pipe even connects to the school?"

"That stink is the same thing I smelled in the school lab," Angie said. "That green stuff has to be some kind of chemical Dippel is leaking into the drains."

Angelo angled his light into the pipe. "She might be right."

Nick edged up beside him. The stink wasn't quite as rank as when they opened the cover, but it was still bad. The pipe was big enough that he could probably walk if he bent a little, but just the idea of going inside freaked him out. He looked at the nearly fluorescent stream of slow-moving water. "Do you think that stuff is dangerous?"

"My guess is that these are old storm drains," Angelo said. "Whatever he's dumping in there is probably diluted by rainwater. I couldn't tell for sure without a microscope."

Carter continued to hold his nose. "I don't care if it's dangerous or not. I'm not going in there. It's dark. It stinks. And who knows what kind of stuff might be crawling around?"

"Would you rather go back?" Angie snarled, whirling to face the rest of them. "Are you going to give up because of a little stink?"

Angelo ran his hands through his hair.

Carter scuffed his shoes on the floor.

"I'll go," Nick said, although he was pretty sure he'd

hurl as soon as he got in the hole.

Dana pressed her lips together before nodding. "I will too."

"Okay." Angelo sighed, his face looking green.

Carter and Tiffany looked at each other before both saying, "Fine," at almost the exact same time, as though neither wanted the other to say it first.

The only one who hadn't agreed was Jake. He was backed as far away from the hole as he could get, shaking his head with a look of disgust. Both of his hands were plastered over his nose.

"It's his superior sense of smell," Angelo said. "If it stinks that bad to us, it must be unbearable for him."

"I guess we could go without him," Dana said.

"No leavsies," the giant cried, swaying back and forth. "No leavsies."

"I think he's afraid to be by himself," Carter said. He stood on his tiptoes to pat Jake's back.

"I don't know what choice we have," Angie said. "The smell will kill him, and he's so big he'd have to crawl through the pipe."

Nick couldn't imagine being on his hands and knees in the filth.

"No leavsies," Jake repeated. "Is not beings to us alonsies." A tear dripped from one of his eyes.

Nick sighed.

"Hang on," Tiffany said. "I have an idea." She unwrapped her silk scarf from her neck, reached into her purse, and pulled out a bottle of perfume. Balling the scarf, she opened the bottle and poured half of its contents onto the silk. Instantly the tunnel was filled with the overwhelming smell of flowers.

"Whoa," Carter said, waving his hands in front of his face. "I think I liked the chemical smell better."

But Jake took his hands from his nose at once and clapped. "Flowersies."

"Yes," Tiffany said. "It smells like flowers. Now kneel down."

Jake knelt beside Tiffany and she wrapped her scarf around his nose and mouth, looping it twice before tying it at the back. "How's that?" she asked.

Jake inhaled, coughed, and said in a voice muted by the scarf, "Pret-ty."

"Good enough," Angie said. "Let's go." Without giving anyone a chance to back out, she entered the hole.

Nick followed behind her. Instantly the smell made him choke.

"Man up," Angie said, splashing ahead of him.

Nick turned on his light and almost wished he hadn't. The walls were covered with a greasy slime that

219

glistened like a putrid rainbow. At the moment, the gunk at the bottom of the pipe barely covered his ankles. But he could see that sometime recently it had been much higher. What if the storm sent a river of sludge rushing down the pipe while they were inside?

Nick was so focused on trying not to barf that he didn't realize Angie had stopped until he ran into her back. "What's wrong?" he asked. "Why did you stop?"

"Is it another dead end?" Dana asked from behind Nick.

Angie shined her light into the darkness ahead. "Get out the bats," she whispered.

Dana handed Nick both of the bats. He kept one and passed the other to Angie. The pipe was just wide enough for him to squeeze up beside her. "What do you see?" he asked.

Angie shook her head. "I didn't *see* anything," she said, her voice so low it was barely more than a breath. "I could have sworn I *heard* something though. Up ahead, in the water."

"What's happening?" Carter called.

"Be quiet, you guys," Nick hissed. He listened intently. Something splashed just out of the range of his light.

"Did you hear it?" Angie asked.

"Yeah," Nick whispered. He held his bat out before him, imagining giant red-eyed rats or snakes big enough to swallow a kid in one bite. He was so focused on staring deep into the tunnel that he didn't notice the creature that climbed out of the water right in front of him until it touched his shoe.

Nick looked down as a pink, five-legged tarantula climbed up his pant leg. "Gahhh!" he screamed, kicking it off. There was something terribly familiar about the spider. Something so horrible he couldn't even process it.

Another spider dropped from the ceiling onto his shoulder. Nick slapped at it, screaming. It felt warm to the touch.

Two more climbed out of the water in front of Angie.

"Don't use the bat in the wat—" Dana started to yell. But she was too late. Angie jabbed her bat at the spider and the electrical current from it ran through the water into everyone standing in it.

It felt like a giant hand lifted Nick and slammed him against the wall of the pipe. A hot metallic taste filled his mouth and the hair on his arms stood straight up.

"Don't use the bats in the water," Dana groaned, trying to stand back up from where the shock had thrown her.

Nick had dropped his flashlight. As he picked it up, he saw one of the big pink spiders floating in the water. It seemed strangely misshapen—all five of its three-jointed legs growing from one side of its body.

Suddenly, he realized what he was seeing. At the same moment he heard a loud splashing coming from the pipe ahead. The creatures—briefly stunned by the bat—had recovered. Dozens of them were racing toward him—hundreds.

"Run!" he screamed. "Go back! Get out!"

Angie stood dazed, the bat hanging loosely in her hand. Nick grabbed her and pulled her back down the pipe. Behind him the splashing was getting closer and closer. Something clawed at his ankle and he stomped on it.

Ahead, he could see the other kids climbing out of the hole. "Get the lid," he yelled. Angie was slowing him down, stumbling like a rag doll, but he knew if he let her go she'd fall. Something clawed at his back. He dropped his bat and slapped it away. Then he was at the opening. Turning. Slipping. Climbing out. Angelo and Dana pulled him and then Angie.

"Close it," he screamed, "before they get out."

A pack of the scrabbling pink creatures spotted the opening and scurried toward it. Just as they were about to break through, Jake picked up the metal lid and heaved it onto the pipe with a deafening clang.

"What kind of s-spiders were those?" Dana stammered, her face white.

"Not spiders," Nick gasped. "Hands."

CHAPTER 25

I'VE GOT TO HAND IT TO THESE KIDS

Nick lay on his back, covered in muck and trying to catch his breath. "How's . . . Angie?"

"She's coming around," Angelo said. "How are you?"

Nick wiped the sweat from his forehead with the back of his arm. "Okay, I think."

Carter leaned over him, his eyes big and round. "When you said hands, you didn't mean actual . . ."

Nick nodded, although he could barely believe it himself. "Severed hands. A hundred of them at least."

"No." Carter shook his head. "That's impossible. I mean, the brain was bad. But hands? Live hands crawling around like spiders?"

"We have to leave," Dana said. "I don't have the weapons to fight something like that."

"No." Angie moaned and sat up. She blinked her eyes and looked around. "We can't go back. Those things had to get into the pipe, so we know it connects to the lab somewhere."

"It doesn't matter," Dana said. "We lost both of our bats and you saw what a bad idea it was to use them in the tunnel anyway."

"Besides," Angelo said, "there aren't enough charges in the bats and fishing poles combined to stop all of those"—he gulped—"hands."

Dana nodded. "We can come back another time. Now that I know what's here I can invent something else to fight them off."

Angie looked at Nick, her eyes begging. "Tell them. Tell them we don't have time to try again."

"If there was any way . . . ," Nick said, feeling like the world's biggest coward.

"There is," Carter said.

He reached into his pillowcase and pulled out the packets of itching powder.

Nick groaned. "Stop kidding around."

"It's not a joke," Carter said. "Dana, give me one of your smoke grenades."

Dana looked at Angelo, who lifted his shoulders. She took one of the cans out of her bag and handed it to Carter. "Be careful with that. If you set it off in here . . ."

"Do I look stupid to you?" Carter asked, then held up a hand. "Don't answer that." He gently peeled part of the duct tape from the can. One by one, he placed the packets around the outside, sealing them on with the tape.

Nick sat up, understanding what Carter was doing. "I think this could really work."

"Itching gas." Dana started to giggle. "How will they scratch themselves?"

Angelo chuckled. "They'll have to ask someone for a . . . a hand."

Angie looked from the grenade to the metal plate. "How do we open and close it fast enough to get the grenade in without the hands escaping?"

Carter turned to Jake. "You can pull up the plate and slam it shut again, right?"

Jake studied the plate. "Opensies. Closeies."

"I think he gets it," Tiffany said.

"You're going to have to pull the tab before he opens the plate or there won't be time to throw it in before the hands escape," Dana said. Even now they could hear fingers scraping and clawing inside the pipe. "If he

226

doesn't get the plate opened in time, you're going to gas us, instead of them."

Carter patted Jake on the knee. "He'll do it."

"If we're going to try it, we might as well get started," Angie said.

Dana wiped her palms on the front of her jeans. "It might be a good idea if the rest of us move back."

Nick punched Carter softly on the shoulder and gave Jake a fist bump. "Good luck, guys." Then he moved a few yards back in the tunnel with the rest of the group.

"Ready to do this thing?" Carter asked.

Jake, who seemed to sense the seriousness of the situation, nodded silently.

"Let's rock those hands then!" Carter yelled, pulling the tab.

Jake reached for the plate. His thick fingers fumbled for the edge.

"One," Dana counted.

"Open the pipe!" Tiffany yelled.

The giant couldn't get a grip on the plate. His fingers kept slipping. Nick saw the problem. The plate had fallen too far in. Its edge was even with the metal of the pipe. There was nothing for Jake to grab.

"Two," Dana whispered. "I don't think he's going to make it."

Nick leaped forward, pulling the knife from his pocket. He pried open the blade just as Dana said, "Three."

Diving toward the opening, Nick rammed the knife at the crack between the plate and the pipe. He missed, and the blade skittered across the metal.

"Get back," Dana screamed. "It's gonna explode!"

"Get rid of the can!" Angie shouted.

Carter clutched the grenade in one hand, eyes locked on Jake's fingers as the giant clawed desperately for the edge of the plate.

Nick tried one more time. His blade found the opening. Knowing it was probably too late, he jammed the knife sidewise. The blade snapped. But the plate slid out half an inch.

Jake's fingers gripped the exposed edge. With a grunt of effort, he grabbed the plate and heaved.

Carter flung his arm forward. His fingers were still on the can when it exploded. White smoke billowed out. Severed hands—somehow sensing the light—crawled toward the opening. Nick lunged at Carter, knocking him away. One of the spider-like hands leaped toward him. Before it could escape, Jake slammed the plate home.

"Are you guys okay?" Angelo said, running to check on Nick and Carter.

Carter flexed his hand. His fingers were red and slightly swollen. "It kind of tingles."

"How long before we can go in?" Angie asked.

Dana calculated on her fingers. "If the smoke takes five minutes to dissipate—and assuming the itching powder will wash off in the water over time—I'd say we wait another three to four minutes."

"What do we do if it didn't work?" Nick asked. The idea of a hundred hands waiting to attack them inside the pipe made his skin crawl.

"Start singing," Angie said. "And hope they clap."

Fortunately, they didn't have to worry about that. As soon as Jake pulled open the plate, he could see the itching powder had done its job. The hands were going crazy. Most of them rolled around in the water, stretching their fingers at awkward angles as they tried to scratch themselves. Some leaped around like crazed frogs. A few rubbed themselves against the side of the pipe, and one pair had even figured out how to scratch each other. It was actually kind of funny if you didn't think about what they were.

None of them paid any attention as Angie, Nick,

229

and the rest of the kids entered the pipe and hurried by. They were careful not to step on any of the hands—the idea of fingers crunching under their feet was too gruesome to consider.

After they had walked about ten minutes, the pipe began to angle up, getting steeper and steeper, until they had to press their hands against the sides to keep from slipping backward. Just as Nick was thinking he couldn't go any farther, the pipe leveled out.

"You okay back there?" he called.

"Either I'm getting used to the stink or I burned out my sense of smell," Carter said.

"Technically, the olfactory system is—" Angelo began.

Angie cut him off. "Over there," she said, pointing. It took Nick a moment to see the dim light she had spotted. "It looks like some kind of grate. Keep your voices down. I think we're close."

Trying not to fall on the slime-coated pipe, they crept up to the grate. There was just enough space between the bars to see what looked like a sort of storage room. It appeared to be empty.

"Help me lift this," Angie said, straining at the bars with both hands.

Nick grabbed the bars and pushed. With a grinding

sound, the grate lifted up and they were able to shove it aside.

Covered with grit and muck, each of the kids climbed out of the pipe. Tiffany plopped down on an empty wooden crate and stared sadly at her feet. "I'm never going to get this out of my shoes."

Nick wasn't sure Jake would be able to make it out of the pipe. His shoulders were so broad, he had to slide one arm up at a time. And even then, it took all of them pulling to get him through the tight opening.

Once they were all up, a deep rumbling vibrated the walls and floor. "It sounds like machinery," Angelo said.

Angie crept to the door and eased it open. "There's a hall outside. The sound seems to be coming from that direction."

"Any more hands?" Nick asked.

Angie shook her head. "I don't see anything at all."

She opened the door the rest of the way, and one by one they entered the hall. "Dippel never showed us this area," Nick whispered as they tiptoed along the stone floor.

"It's got to be the hidden basement," Dana said.

They stopped where the hall split into a T, checking to make sure there was no one in sight. Angelo frowned. "It's weird there are no guards here."

"Maybe they're all outside," Angie suggested. "Dippel probably never thought anyone would make it this far."

Dana pointed to the left. "The sound's coming from that way."

"What's the weird light?" Carter said. An odd purple pulsing illuminated the far end of the walls.

Angie started walking. "Only one way to find out."

Nick hesitated before following. His gut told him it couldn't be this easy.

"Coming?" Carter asked.

Nick nodded and hurried after Angie. As they moved farther down the hall, they could see that it ended in a right-hand turn. The closer they got to the corner, the louder the sound grew. It had a consistent pulsing to it, *rurrr-rurrr-rurrr*, that appeared to match the flickering of the purple light.

"I think we're close," Dana said. Pausing a few feet from the corner, she handed out the bats they'd recovered from the pipe, and the fishing poles. There were only enough weapons for five of them.

"You guys take them," Angelo said, taking his PROG from his backpack. "That machinery has an electrical sound to it. I may need my hands free."

Angie licked her lips. "Everyone ready?"

Nick looked back at Jake. The giant was cowering several feet back, his hands and legs shaking.

"He doesn't like this place," Carter said.

Nick rubbed his hands across his arms. The air down here was damp and cold. But it was more than that. There was a feeling of evil here. Of something so old and wrong that it had been absorbed by the very stone of the walls.

"Let's go," Angie whispered. Holding a fishing pole, she slipped around the corner.

Nick was right behind her, bat in hand. Neither of them took more than a single step before freezing at the sight before them.

Twenty feet away, the hall opened into a huge, circular room. At its center, a silver two-tiered pedestal rose high into the air. At the top of the pedestal, Dippel sat behind the controls of what looked like some bizarre mishmash of a giant ray gun from a science-fiction movie and a high-tech electrical control panel.

On the base, about two feet off the ground, a purple orb of electricity hissed and shot out sparks. Across from the ball was something so repulsive, Nick's mind refused to accept what he was seeing.

A quivering blob ten feet across appeared to be

233

made of dozens of bodies combined like the pieces of a jigsaw puzzle. It was neither man nor animal, but some twisted mutation of both. Nick could see horns and fur mixed in with feet and hands. Eyes, some big, others small, blinked among random ears, mouths, and noses. He thought several of the faces were either laughing or screaming, but they were so twisted he couldn't be sure.

Sticking out from the blob were crazy pieces of electronics. Circuit boards, transformers, switches, normal electrical outlets like you'd plug a toaster into. Cords and cables connected to the electronics and disappeared into the blob's flesh.

Surrounding the pedestal were twenty or thirty of Dippel's football players. They were protected in the orb, marching in a series of precise—almost military—movements.

In and amongst them, random body parts crawled, marched, and hopped. Severed legs stepped side by side. Arms slapped the ground, dragged themselves forward across the floor, reached out, and slapped again. Individual fingers crawled like worms, slipping and sliding forward.

Dippel stared down at the purple ball. It took a

moment for Nick to understand why. Trapped inside the purple fire—arms and legs spread—was a person. It was Cody Gills. His eyes were open and his mouth was stretched wide in a soundless scream.

CHAPTER 26

I'M AFRAID THIS CHAPTER KEPT ME UP AT NIGHT

Silently, Nick, Angie, and the others backed around the corner.

"What *is* that thing?" Nick asked, when he could finally catch his breath.

Dana opened her mouth but no words came out.

"This is . . ." Nick held out his hands, unable to come up with the right words to describe such an abomination.

Angie turned to Angelo, who was still gripping his electronic box. "Can that thing of yours free Cody?"

Angelo chewed his lower lip. "Maybe. If I could get to that purple ball. There's no way to know for sure."

"How could we get past the football players?" Tiffany asked. "They're huge."

"How many can we take out with your weapons?" Angie asked Dana.

Dana shook her head. "No more than fifteen. And that's if we had time to cast and reel in all of the poles until they are out of charges. Which we don't. Besides, do you see those formations he's got them in? We saw how much luck the Rams had getting past that line at the football game. We'd be lucky if we could take out a third of them before they overran us."

Nick clenched his fists. They were so close. If only they could get more help. He looked at Tiffany. "Your cell phone. You can call for help."

Tiffany shook her head and took her phone out of her purse to show him. "No bars. But I haven't had any service since we entered the maintenance tunnel. Either Dippel's blocking transmission or we're too far underground."

Angie darted her eyes around the hallway, searching for a solution. "We have to come up with a distraction."

"Great," Nick said. "And where are we going to find that?"

Carter looked up from his pillowcase with a strange

grin on his face, put his finger to his chest, and said, "You can call me Mr. Distraction."

• • •

Fifteen minutes later, Carter was balanced on Jake's shoulders. His pillowcase—now loaded down with the rest of Dana's smoke grenades—hung from his left hand.

"Are you sure about this?" Nick asked.

The giant was shaking so badly he looked like an overgrown scarecrow caught in a tornado.

Carter squeezed Jake's shoulder. "You can do it, right, buddy?"

Jake wrung his hands together, sighed, and nodded. "Rightsies, bud-dy."

"Take your positions," Angie said.

Nick stepped behind and to the left of Jake while Angie stood across from him on the right, each of them holding a fishing pole. Dana stood behind and to the left of Nick, holding a bat while Tiffany stood off to her right with a pole. Together they formed an inverted *V* with Jake and Carter at the tip of the formation.

Inside the wedge, Angelo gripped his PROG in one hand and a bat in the other.

"Remember," Angie said, "the bat is for self-defense

only. Your number-one job is to blow the electronics."

"Okay," Angelo said, his voice dry and gravelly.

Up on the pedestal, Dippel moved the laser gun. It now pointed at Cody. The purple ball had sprouted a funnel on one side, and a stream of some kind of energy was flowing between the funnel and the blob creature.

"Looks like he's about to start the transfer," Angelo said.

"We're not going to give him the chance," Angie said. She looked up at Carter. "Time for the diversion."

Carter reached into his pillowcase and pulled out the bottle of aftershave. He twisted off the lid, took a sniff, and wrinkled his nose. "If this doesn't scare them off, nothing will."

Jake put a hand to the scarf covering his nose.

"Hey, over there!" Carter shouted. Dippel looked up from his equipment—pink eyes flashing. "Get a whiff of this." Carter reached back like a quarterback throwing a Hail Mary and heaved the bottle high into the air. It landed on the ground a few feet from the base of the pedestal and smashed open, splashing the pungent blue aftershave everywhere. All of the creatures in the vicinity that had noses clapped their hands to their faces and backed away, trying to escape the stench.

"Get them!" Dippel shouted, electricity shooting

239

from his hands and the bolts on the sides of his jaw. "Thirty-four cross wing right."

At their master's words, the football players began to fall into offensive formation. But Carter was already pulling smoke grenades from his pillowcase, yanking the tabs, and throwing them as fast as he could.

"Charge!" Angie yelled, firing her fishing pole as billows of purple-and-yellow smoke filled the room.

Two hulking linebackers came charging out of the smoke. Nick aimed at the first one and fired. The hooks caught on one of the runners' legs, and Nick triggered a bolt of electricity that sent it skidding to the ground.

The second one managed to hit Dana with a forearm, spinning her around. "Take this!" she screamed, zapping him with her bat. His eyes snapped wide open and he spun halfway around before collapsing.

It was hard to tell what was happening after that. Monsters ran past with their hands over their noses, fleeing the stench of Carter's dad's aftershave. Nick retrieved his hooks and fired again at an arm that reached for him. Tiffany zapped a blocker that must have been seven feet tall and nearly as wide.

Eight severed hands came scrambling toward them, but Carter's feathers must have tickled their palms, because they quickly backed away. "There are more

240

where those came from," he yelled, throwing another handful from his down pillow.

Two snarling linemen tried to tackle Jake and Carter. "Block!" Carter yelled, and Jake threw a forearm that sent them reeling. "Feel the pain!" Carter yelled. He seemed to be having the time of his life.

The smoke swirled and the silver pedestal came into view. Angelo ducked a block, jumped a flock of crawling fingers, and leaped onto the base.

"On your right!" Tiffany shouted as a player who must have been the quarterback picked up a beaker and flung it at Angelo. Angelo ducked just in time and the beaker shattered against a wall.

Angelo spun and lunged at the purple ball. Streams of electricity zapped the platform all around him. Miraculously, he managed to reach the orb without being hit. He switched on the PROG, grabbed the alligator clips—one in each hand—and rammed them into the purple fire.

Lightning exploded from the ball like shards of metal from a bomb. The low rumble of the machine changed to a deafening screech. The ball went from purple to blinding white and then flashed off.

Everything went black as the power grid shut down. Nick blinked, unable to believe what had just happened.

241

In the darkness Angie screamed a victory roar.

They'd done it! They'd knocked out Dippel's device. It was incredible. Blindly Nick stumbled forward, feeling for the metal platform. Now they had to find a way to get Cody and escape from the school.

But just as Nick's fingers found the platform, the rumbling started up again. Deeper than before, rougher. The lights flickered and came back on. The purple orb sputtered and reformed. Angelo got to his knees, his PROG a charred ruin, the cables melted.

From above came an insane cackling. Dr. Dippel raised both arms, sparks dancing across his fingers as he shouted, "Perhaps you've never heard of backup generators!"

CHAPTER 27

THIS IS THE POINT WHERE YOU SAY, "JUST KIDDING!"

As the smoke cleared away, the football players began returning. Nick aimed his fishing pole at a muscular linebacker who lumbered toward him. But when he pushed the button on the side of the reel, the hooks barely even sparked and the creature tore the pole from his hands and ripped it to pieces.

Four hands crawled out and began mopping up the aftershave.

Angie held her weapon in front of her as though it were still dangerous, even though it was clear she was out of energy as well. Dana cradled her right arm to her chest.

Carter—out of grenades—let his last handful of feathers float to the ground, then slumped forward on Jake's shoulders.

Tiffany sniffed and wiped away a tear.

"Why so sad?" Dippel asked gleefully. He pointed toward the orb, where Cody was struggling. "You are about to witness a once-in-a-lifetime occurrence." The mad scientist chuckled. "Well, since I'll be doing the same thing to each of you after I'm done with your friend, I suppose it's not strictly *once* in a lifetime."

"Leave him alone!" Angie growled.

Dippel conjured a crackling blue ball from thin air and tossed it from one hand to another. "I like your fire, young lady. I think I'll feed you to my pet next."

Nick's head dropped. No one knew where they were. And even if someone figured out where they'd gone, all they'd find was a school closed for Thanksgiving break. There was no way out of this mess.

Dippel pointed at Jake. "*You* I am most disappointed in. You've been very disobedient and must be punished." He sent a lightning bolt from his finger that crashed to the floor in front of Jake's feet, and the giant backed away moaning and shaking.

Carter climbed down from Jake's shoulders and

244

stepped in front of him—hands balled into fists. "Leave him alone!"

"Enough!" Dippel roared. "I tire of your bravado. We'll see how courageous you are when it's your turn." He gestured to his team. "Bring them forward."

The football players surrounded Nick and his friends, driving them until they were standing at the very edge of the platform. Jake covered his face in his hands, trembling in terror.

Dippel did something to the device in front of him and the orb sparked and began to stretch toward the blob. Hands and legs on the blob quivered, reaching toward the ball. Angelo pushed himself away to the edge of the base.

Cody's back arched. His mouth opened as though he was screaming, but no sound came out.

The Pale One cackled. "Behold what men have only dreamed of until now. Capturing what only the gods have controlled." Blue fire danced around his body— shooting from the bolts on the sides of his face and crackling from the tips of his wild white hair. "All my prior creations required electrical recharges to stay animated. But, this, this will be my masterpiece. I am giving true life!"

245

Dippel moved a lever and the funnel on the side of the orb grew and stretched until a white beam of energy shot out from Cody to the monstrosity. The mouths on the creature opened and closed hungrily and Nick thought he saw the blob begin to swell.

"Stop it," Angie screamed. "You're killing him."

"Not technically," the mad scientist said. "Although I must admit, once I'm through with him, it will be hard to tell the difference."

The throbbing sound of the generators increased and a dark green line spread along the white beam, drawing energy from Cody into the blob.

Nick watched in horror as Cody strained against the force holding him. Whatever the green stuff was, it seemed to be exciting the blob. Its eyes opened wide. Limbs waved. It was definitely growing. At the same time, Cody began to wilt.

Nick looked at his friends' reflections in the side of the silver pedestal. Dana appeared to be in shock. Angelo looked defeated. Carter buried his face against the side of Jake's leg.

Even Jake's terror had turned to surrender. He stared blankly at the ground, one hand resting on Carter's head, the other hanging limply at his side. His body, so broad and strong before, appeared bent and drawn in, as though whatever was being taken from Cody was being taken from him at the same time.

The beam running between Cody and the blob had turned completely green, pumping like a hose under full pressure. The blob expanded like a water balloon being filled.

"We have to do something," Angie hissed.

The green stuff had to be Cody's life force. And it was nearly gone. This was beyond evil. It went against every part of human nature.

Nick had to find a way to stop it. But how? If he went near the orb, wouldn't the creature just absorb his animus too? He looked from Cody—the last bits of his life force being sucked away—to the engorged blob, and the image reminded him of something Carter had said once about a mosquito. An idea came to him. It was crazy, and incredibly dangerous. But it was the only way he could think of to stop Dippel, and maybe save Cody.

The creature quivered and appeared to pucker as the final bits of green slid out of Cody, like a kid sipping the last of his soda from a straw. It was now or never. Nick jumped on the platform and ran toward the purple orb.

"Get away from there!" Angelo yelled. He tried to

grab Nick's arm. "That thing will kill you."

But Nick had already made up his mind. He ducked out of Angelo's reach, gritted his teeth, and leaped at the ball of energy.

The result was immediate. Nick slammed against the side of the orb like a piece of metal pulled to a magnet. The whine from the machinery soared, as loud as a jet engine revving. To Nick it felt like a hand plunged into the middle of his stomach, wrapped itself around his guts, and pulled.

The energy beam gushed with green and the blob sucked it greedily up.

Out of the corner of his eye, Nick saw Angie cover her face with her hands.

Dippel laughed insanely. "Couldn't wait your turn?" He shoved the lever higher.

"What are you doing?" Carter screamed.

Nick could feel something vital being pulled from him. The blob continued to swell, but it wasn't going to be enough. Using all of his strength, he managed to utter one word. "Mosquito."

Carter's eyes widened with recognition.

"He's killing himself," Tiffany sobbed.

"No," Carter said. "He's trying to kill the blob. He's

trying to pop it like a mosquito."

"Yes." Angelo nodded. "He's trying to overload it like I did with the electronics. Only he's using his own animus instead of electricity." He looked at the power beam, which was already starting to turn back to white. "He doesn't have enough."

"We've got to help him!" Carter screamed. Without a second thought, he raced toward the ball, grabbed Nick's hand, and flung himself forward. The sound raised another notch as the beam filled with green.

"Come . . . on," Carter groaned, his body twisting against the ball.

Angelo hesitated for only a second before grabbing Nick's other hand and pressing against the orb. Nick could feel their life forces join with his.

For the first time, Dippel appeared concerned. "Stop that," he shouted. "One at a time." He yanked on the lever, trying to slow down the flow. But it had no effect. Presented with so much energy, the blob expanded like a balloon. It was nearly twice the size as when they'd first seen it, and still growing.

Dana was the first of the girls to grasp what was happening. "Let's go," she said, taking Angie's hand. "Let's blow this thing up like an overinflated beach ball." Together the two of them ran to the orb. Dana grabbed Angelo's hand as she and Angie slammed against the ball.

The energy beam was nearly a foot in diameter now—bright green with animus.

"Tiffany." Carter managed to pull one arm free from the ball. "You know you've always wanted to hold my hand."

"In your dreams." Tiffany wiped the tears from her eyes, brushed back a lock of hair, and jumped onto the platform, where she took Carter's hand.

At the top of the pedestal, circuits were overheating. Smoke flowed from several boards. "Stop it!" Dippel screamed. He clawed at switches and levers, but it was clear things had gone beyond his control. "You can't do this!"

Carter lifted his head so he was looking straight into the mad scientist's eyes and grunted, "Bite me."

Nick had never felt anything like this in his life. It was as if he, Carter, Angelo, Dana, Angie, and Tiffany had been fused into one powerful organism. An incredible sense of awareness filled his body. But just as quickly it began to drain away. On the other side of the platform, the blob was massive. Cables smoked and outlets threw out green sparks. It was clear it was on the verge of bursting.

But the green power beam was starting to narrow. The last of their animus was draining away and it wasn't going to be quite enough. If only they had one more person.

It was almost as though Carter and Tiffany read his mind. Maybe they did. Maybe the fusing of their life forces gave them some kind of limited telepathy. Both of them turned and looked toward Jake, who was cowering as close to the platform as the football players would allow—his hands over his eyes.

"Help . . . us," Carter groaned.

"Handsies," Tiffany cried weakly.

Dippel glared at the giant, pointing at him with an electric blue finger. "Don't you dare. I command you to stay away from them."

"Help-sies." Carter's voice was nearly gone.

Nick could feel the last of the animus being sucked out of him. Things began to turn gray.

Jake looked from Dippel to Tiffany.

"You are my creation!" Dippel screamed. "You will obey me."

Tiffany raised her hand slowly. Her fingers just touched her hair. "Pret-ty," she whispered.

Jake touched his own hair. His eyes widened. His

nostrils flared. "Pret-ty!" he growled.

"Tackle him!" Dippel commanded his team.

A line of hulking players raced toward Jake just like they'd done against the football teams Dippel had trained them against.

Three of them grabbed at Jake. He ducked his shoulder, sending two of them flying, and spun around the third in a move that would have left a football crowd screaming with excitement. Jake ran for the pedestal, but two more players stepped in front of him. He faked right, then ducked left, leaving them in his dust.

There were only two more players between Jake and the pedestal, but they were huge—their faces masks of determination. Jake ducked low, like he was going to dive between them. When they responded by lowering their shoulders, Jake grabbed both of their heads in his palms and slammed them together like a pair of coconuts.

Both players collapsed to the ground as Dippel screamed in frustration.

"Touchdown!" Jake roared. He vaulted onto the platform and stepped between Angie and Carter, taking each of their hands.

The machinery, which had started to wind back down, screamed to a frenzied pitch. Nick felt a burst of childlike innocence flow through him. A ball of green animus blasted from the purple orb into the creature. Cody's eyes flipped open.

The blob quivered. Its wet pink skin stretched. And then it exploded into a million pieces and everything went black.

CHAPTER 28

WHAT WE NEED NOW IS A VISIT FROM SOMEONE TALL, DARK, AND HANDSOME

Waking up was like swimming out of a deep pit filled with thick, black tar. Nick tried to sit up and immediately the room began to swirl. A hand pushed him gently back down.

"Give it a moment," a familiar voice said.

He looked up to see a pair of piercing black eyes studying him. He'd seen the face before. The light skin. The dark, slicked-back hair. "Mr. Blackham?"

The librarian nodded.

Nick tried sitting up again. This time more slowly. His head felt like a cannonball attached to his shoulders. He could barely keep it upright. Carter, Angelo, and the others were sitting on nearby cots. They looked like they had just woken up as well. "Other than Cody, you had the most energy drained," Mr. Blackham said. "It will take you the longest to recover completely."

Nick blinked. "Where are we?" he asked.

Mr. Blackham stepped away from the cot where Nick had been resting, pulled across a chair, and took a seat. "You are on the main level of the school."

Nick recognized the dormitory from the tour he'd taken.

"How did you find us?" Angelo asked, standing shakily up from his bed and coming over.

The librarian shot him an amused glance. "I've discovered it's wise to keep an eye on you three." He looked to where Angie, Dana, and Tiffany were sitting on a nearby bed, whispering. "Make that six."

"I thought you were out of the country," Nick said.

"I was." Mr. Blackham rubbed his chin. "I've been tracking Dippel since he arrived. I wasn't sure what he was up to. But as soon as I heard about the missing bodies, I put two and two together. I had a feeling you'd investigate, so I called the library to give you a few clues." He gave a pained laugh. "I also said to make sure you didn't do anything until you spoke to me. Apparently that message wasn't delivered."

"Where is Dippel?" Nick asked, terror filling his chest.

"We've placed him where he can't hurt anyone else," Mr. Blackham said, crossing his legs.

"*We?*" For the first time, Nick realized there were other people in the room with them. Men and women—all of them dressed in the same long black coats and gloves—hurried in and out of the room, carrying bags and boxes. They all had the same slick dark hair and pallid complexions. Several of them wore sunglasses, although the room was very dim.

"Who are these people?" Nick asked.

"Just some fellow . . . librarians." Mr. Blackham uncrossed his legs and stood.

"Librarians?" Nick was pretty sure these people didn't work in any library. Before he could ask more, though, Angie, Dana, and Tiffany walked over.

"Are you all right?" Angie asked.

Nick rubbed the back of his neck. All of his muscles ached like he'd been stuck in a bag and rolled down a steep, rocky hill. "I think so."

"Let's get you on your feet," Mr. Blackham said, pulling Nick up. "It's time for you kids to be heading home."

"We're just going to leave? What will the police say

when they find . . ." Angie waved her hands as though she didn't have enough words to describe everything they'd seen that night.

Mr. Blackham pulled on his gloves and gave a small smile. "When the authorities arrive, they will find a rather mysteriously empty school. There will no doubt be some talk concerning the disappearance of Mr. Dippel and his students. But nothing more . . . *unusual* . . . than that."

Nick realized someone was missing. "Where's Cody?"

"Being cared for," the librarian said. "When he regains consciousness it will be better if he remembers none of this."

"So he's going back to those terrible grandparents of his?" Angie scowled.

Mr. Blackham tilted his chin ever so slightly. "It would be nice if he had some friends to help lift his burdens."

Angie nodded.

"What about Jake?" Carter asked.

Mr. Blackham shook his head.

Nick's throat shut tight. He couldn't breathe.

Carter's face went white. A tear ran down his cheek. "He's . . . *dead*?"

"No," the librarian said, gripping his shoulder. "I'm sorry. I didn't mean to frighten you. All of Dippel's creations will be cared for, I assure you. We are finding an especially good home for Jake."

"I'm gonna miss Jake," Carter said.

"Yeah," Tiffany agreed. "He turned out to be a pretty awesome guy."

Mr. Blackham steered them down the hall and out the front door. "What the seven of you did was amazing. Incredibly stupid but amazing. If you had possessed just a hair less life force, Dippel's monstrosity would have been powerful beyond belief and we would be looking for homes for *you*." He glanced down at Nick. "How did you know it would work?"

Nick shrugged. "I didn't."

The librarian laughed. After all the horror they'd been through, it was a good sound. "Sometimes ignorance really is bliss. But you know, combining your life forces like that can never be completely undone. There will always be a part of Jake in all of you. Just like there will always be a bit of your life force in each of your friends, and theirs in you."

Tiffany looked at Carter and put her hand over her mouth. "I think I'm going to be sick."

Mr. Blackham chuckled. "Get some rest. You deserve

it. By the way, I hear you boys are going camping next week."

"Yeah," Nick said. "With my parents. How did you know that?"

Mr. Blackham tapped his eyes with two fingers. "Keep your eyes open. The woods can be an interesting place."

Nick wasn't sure he liked the sound of that. But before he could say anything more, Mr. Blackham turned and walked away. The kids walked down the hill toward the train station.

"You know," Angie said, "just because we saved your butts this time, don't expect us to hang around with you dweebs."

"Saved *us*?" Nick said. "Who's the one who came up with the idea to blow up the blob?"

"Who got you there in the first place?" Angie said. "If it wasn't for us, you boys would still be sitting at home."

"If it wasn't for Angelo's A.S.T. device, you wouldn't have found the wrapper."

"He never could have used it if my mom hadn't let us in the morgue."

Dana and Angelo just grinned.

Nick leaned over to Angelo and whispered, "Are

259

you and Dana . . . you know? Because if you are, I guess I could live with it."

Angelo punched him on the shoulder. "Absolutely not."

Nick wasn't sure if he was telling the truth or not. But maybe it didn't matter. Change was okay. As long as it wasn't *too* much.

Tiffany pulled out her phone and started texting.

Angelo opened his notebook and began writing.

Carter scratched the back of his head, where the hair was just starting to grow back in to cover up the ram. "Anybody feel like stopping for a burger on the way home?"

Nick grinned. Some things would always stay the same.

Until Next
We Meet

Well, that was a bit too close for an old librarian like me. I thought you promised to keep an eye on the boys—and girls—while I was gone.

Then again, I might have known someone like you couldn't resist a good mystery. Especially if that mystery involves creepy crawlies, nightmare creatures, and power-hungry mad scientists. I don't imagine I could have resisted that at your age either.

Fortunately everyone seems to have survived . . . this time. But let me warn you now. This is not the end of dark happenings in Pleasant Hill. Things are only going to get stranger, more terrifying, and more dangerous.

Perhaps it might be better if you took up a slightly less stressful hobby than monster hunting. Say, knitting baby socks, or collecting the cardboard tubes inside toilet-paper rolls. Have a nice glass of hot cocoa. Read a book of poems. And whatever you do, if something knocks on your door late at night, do NOT let it in. Especially if it looks familiar.

Sincerely,

B. B.

TURN THE PAGE
FOR A FRIGHTENING
FIRST LOOK AT. . .

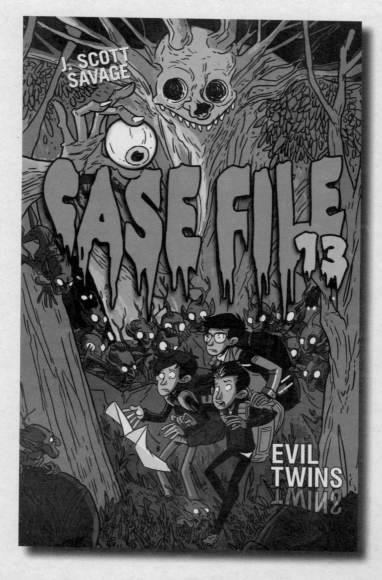

CHAPTER 1

SETTING SAIL . . .
OR SHOULD IT
BE DRIVE?
BE DRIVE?

Saturday morning was the perfect day for a campout. The sky was blue and, although it was early December, the temperature was nearly sixty-five degrees. Nick and his friends Carter and Angelo had been looking forward to this trip ever since Nick's dad announced it. But now Nick was afraid the trip was going to end before it even got started. Mom was digging through the gear in the back of the car like a cat hunting a mouse, while Dad complained from the driveway behind her.

"Did you bring the sleeping bags?" Mom asked, pushing aside a stack of air mattresses.

"Of course," Dad said, hands on his hips.

"First-aid box?"

"Complete with snakebite kit, instant ice packs, and suture set."

Mom looked through a grocery bag, set it aside, and examined every canteen individually.

"Is she always like this?" Carter whispered.

Nick stepped away from the SUV so his parents couldn't overhear him. "Dad's got kind of a reputation for forgetting things when we go camping."

Angelo pushed his new glasses up on his nose and peered toward the car. "What *kinds* of things?"

"Well, once he brought a whole bunch of fancy dehydrated food but nothing to cook it in."

"How bad could that be?" Carter asked, dumping a pack of cherry Pop Rocks into his mouth.

Nick made a face. "Ever tried sucking on a mouthful of dried shrimp Rangoon, waiting for it to get soft enough that you could chew it? Trust me, it's not pretty. Another time he packed the tent but forgot the spikes. In the middle of the night, this freak storm picked up the tent and rolled us all down the side of a hill into a lake."

Angelo's eyes widened in alarm. "Maybe I'll go help your mom check on things."

Carter stuck out his tongue to make the candy in his mouth pop louder. Red-colored saliva splashed from

2

his mouth with each pop.

"Dude, stop spitting," Nick said. "That's disgusting. And what's with the hair?" Carter was always changing his hair color. One month it was neon green, the next it was blue. But this was the first time he'd ever dyed it black with white down the middle.

"Zebra stripes," Carter said, swallowing the Pop Rocks. "Tell me it's not the coolest yet."

"*It's not the coolest yet,*" Nick repeated. "I hate to tell you, dude, but you look like a skunk."

"That's cool too," Carter said, opening another bag of Pop Rocks. "Are we still planning on making s'mores?"

"Yeah," Nick said. "We're making s'mores. I made sure Dad packed the marshmallows, graham crackers, and chocolate." Sometimes he wondered if Carter was able to stop thinking about food for more than a minute or two at a time.

"Well?" Dad asked, holding his hands palms up as Mom climbed from the back of the car. "Are you ready to apologize and admit I didn't forget anything this time?"

Mom brushed her hands on the front of her jeans. "I'm not apologizing until we actually set up camp. But I can't see anything you missed."

"Never doubt genius," Dad said, closing the hatch. "Let's go, everybody. It's time to set sail on the adventure of a lifetime."

"I think we've had *more* than enough adventures to last a lifetime," Mom muttered under her breath. "I'd settle for a nice, normal campout."

"*Normal?*" Dad grinned, clearly elated by his victory. "Were Lewis and Clark satisfied with normal? Did Cortés want a simple campout? Was Magellan scared of a little adventure?"

Angelo scratched the back of his head. "Actually, Magellan was killed by natives."

Dad scowled. "Get in the car."

"How come I have to sit in the middle?" Carter complained as the three boys slid onto the back bench seat.

"You're the shortest," Angelo said.

Carter snorted. "Short people get no respect."

Nick's dad started the car and pulled out of the driveway as Mom programmed the GPS.

"Where's the campground?" Angelo asked.

"Near Santa Cruz." Mom craned her neck to look back at the boys. "I'm so excited to see the tide pools."

"The tide pools are fascinating," Angelo said. "And the monarch butterflies should be there for their winter migration."

Angelo never failed to surprise Nick with his knowledge. Of course he knew everything there was to know about monsters, monster movies, alien abductions, and anything else paranormal. It was what had drawn the Three Monsterteers, as they called themselves, together in the first place. But he seemed to know about everything else, too.

"*Butterflies?*" Carter scoffed. "I'm planning on catching a mermaid. I brought a couple of Almond Joys. Mermaids go crazy for coconut."

Nick's mom rolled her eyes and turned to face the front.

"Where did you hear that?" Angelo asked.

Carter shifted in his seat and pulled a small booklet out of his back pocket. "Right here." He opened the book, which was called *Finding and Catching the Lovelies of the Sea.* "Mermaids are vegetarians by nature," he read, "living primarily off of seaweed and algae. However, they have been known to crawl onto shore for a rare treat of fresh coconut."

Angelo opened his monster notebook and started writing, but Nick shook his head. "What would you do with a mermaid if you caught one?"

"Drop out of school and take her on the road," Carter said at once, as though he'd been giving it a lot

5

of thought. "Do you have any idea what people would pay to see a live mermaid? I'd probably have to teach her to do stuff. You know, like card tricks, or juggling flaming chain saws."

"I dated a mermaid once," Dad said as he pulled onto the freeway. "Things went swimmingly at first. Then her scales starting rubbing me the wrong way and—" Mom cut him off with a stare, and he quickly changed the subject. "Wait till you boys see my new camp stove. It's a beauty. Three burners, adjustable windscreen. It even has a built-in cook timer."

Angelo nodded, clearly impressed. "What kind of fuel does it take?"

"*Fuel?*" Dad's face went white as he looked toward the back of the car.

"Tell me you didn't forget fuel for the stove," Mom said.

Dad braked, hung his head, and got off at the next exit.

CHAPTER 2

THIS IS WHY YOU SHOULDN'T READ— OR GORGE YOURSELF—ON CURVY ROADS

"Here's the thing I don't get," Nick said as his dad steered up the winding Highway 17 through the Santa Cruz Mountains. They'd been driving for just over an hour and were less than thirty minutes from the beach. "If a vampire bit a mummy, would the mummy turn into a vampire, stay a mummy, or form some weird combination?"

"Definitely stay a mummy," Angelo answered without even stopping to think about it. "Mummies don't have any blood for the vampire to infect."

"Sure. I get that. But does it have to infect the blood? I mean, couldn't the vampire just inject his venom into the mummy's flesh and turn its mummy

7

cells into vampire cells?"

Angelo shook his head. "Assuming we're talking about a sanguivore—the kind of vampire that feeds off blood, not energy—vampires suck in blood from the victim, mix it with their venom, and kind of spit it back out. The blood is how the venom mixes into the rest of the victim's body. Sort of like what Carter does with food. Except he never spits out anything he eats."

Carter gave him a dirty look. "I'm right here, you know."

Nick considered Angelo's words for a minute, staring out the window at the dense forest passing by outside. "Then if a mummy and a vampire got into a fight, I would totally bet on the mummy. They have supernatural strength and excellent endurance. Plus, they are immune to pain and have all kinds of cool curses."

"Not all mummies have curses," Angelo said, flipping through his monster notebook. "And even if they do, the curses might not work on vampires. More importantly, vampires can fly, and they are much smarter than mummies."

Nick smirked. "How can you possibly know that?"

"Simple." Angelo pointed to a picture of a long hook in his notebook. "Mummies don't have any brains. When the embalmers prepare the body, they shove this

8

through his nose and—"

"That's disgusting," Mom said, spinning around to glare at the boys from the front seat of the car. "Can't you think of something fun to do until we get to the campsite? When I was a girl we used to sing songs while we drove."

Dad grinned back at them in the rearview mirror. "'Ninety-Nine Bottles of Beer on the Wall' was one of my favorites."

Nick wrinkled his nose. "So you'd rather have us sing a repetitive verse about an alcoholic beverage we won't even be able to legally drink for ten more years ninety-nine times?"

"No!" Mom exploded, giving Dad the evil eye. "Why don't you play a game? You can look for the letters of the alphabet on license plates."

"No offense," Nick said, "but I think I'd rather watch my fingernails grow."

Mom frowned. "All right. How about I Spy?"

"That could be fun," Angelo said. He looked out the window for a minute. "I spy something with sharp fangs and snakes for hair."

"A gorgon," Nick said. "That was easy." He looked out his window. "I spy something with four legs and the head and wings of an eagle."

9

"Trick question. If all four legs are lion legs, it's an opinicus. But if the front legs are aquiline, like an eagle's, it's a griffin. Of course if the back legs are . . ."

Mom turned away with a sigh, muttering something that sounded like "Why couldn't I have given birth to a girl?"

Carter, who had been going through snacks as if he hadn't eaten in a week, looked up from the mermaid book he'd been reading and wiped his forehead. "Are we going to be on this curvy road for long?"

"Do you feel sick?" Mom asked.

"A little," Carter said. His stomach gurgled so loudly it sounded like a milk shake in a blender.

Nick studied his friend's face. "You do look sort of pale."

"Look straight ahead," Dad said. "You don't want to throw up. Once, when I was a kid, my dad drove us up this majorly curvy road. That made my stomach feel sort of queasy. But then he fed us these smelly meat chunks that turned out to be eel jerky, and—"

Carter's face turned from white to green. "Pull over," he said, clutching his hands to his mouth.

Nick's father pulled the car off the highway, and before Nick could even get his seat belt off, Carter was scrambling over him and clawing for the door handle.

"Eel jerky? *Really*?" Mom groaned, shaking her head. "You tell a sick boy about the time your sadistic father fed you *eel jerky*?"

Dad held out his hands. "He didn't let me get to the end of my story. It turned out that even though the eel jerky smelled terrible it made my stomach feel much better. Or was that the Pepto-Bismol my mom gave me? Come to think of it, the eel might have . . ." He glanced out the window to where Carter was gagging on the side of the road. "Maybe you better go help Carter. I think he just threw up an armchair."

"You. Are. Impossible," Mom said before getting out of the car.

Dad looked back at Nick and Angelo. "There was another song we used to sing about a kid who eats a bad peanut and dies. But that might not be the best song either."

A few minutes later, Carter climbed into his seat, sipping from a bottle of water Nick's mom had given him.

Mom got back into the car, slamming her door so hard it rattled the drink in her cup holder. She looked at the boys. "Until we get to the campground, no food, no reading, and no disgusting stories. Clear?"

"Yes," the boys answered together.

11

"Roll down both of your windows a little so Carter can get some fresh air. And you," she said, looking at Dad. "Drive slower, stop suggesting inappropriate songs, and no more stories of any kind."

Dad opened his mouth as if he was going to argue, but then he thought better of it and restarted the car.

"Feeling better?" Nick asked as they pulled onto the freeway.

"I guess," Carter said. "Man, it felt like my gut was trying to turn inside out." He wiped his mouth with the back of his hand. "Actually I feel pretty good now."

"Not surprising." Angelo glanced up at Nick's mom before whispering, "Getting sick to your stomach feels gross because your body is telling you not to do whatever made you sick in the first place. Throwing up releases endorphins that make you feel better so the vomiting doesn't seem as bad."

Nick groaned. "Who knows stuff like that? What do you do, study books about puking?"

"I study books about everything," Angelo said in a tone of voice that made it clear he couldn't understand why everyone didn't do the same. "You never know when something will come in handy. Say an alien abducts you and makes you eat poison. Knowing when to puke and when not to could make all the difference."

12

Mom started to turn around and the boys quieted down.

"Speaking of aliens," Carter whispered. "When I was, you know, yakking, something weird happened."

"Please don't tell me your puke formed the shape of a flying saucer," Nick said. A couple of years before, Carter had gotten on a kick where everything formed some kind of symbol. Clouds looked like werewolves, trees looked like dragons. Nick and Angelo finally put a stop to it when he wanted to describe the shapes of things that really shouldn't be discussed.

"No," Carter said. "Although now that you mention it . . ."

Angelo held up a finger. "Don't go there."

"Fine," Carter said. "Besides, that's not what I wanted to tell you."

"What *did* you want to tell us?" Angelo asked, twirling one hand impatiently.

Carter waved Nick and Angelo closer. "Okay. When I was throwing up—which actually looked more like a pepperoni pizza than a flying saucer—I think something was watching me from just inside the woods."

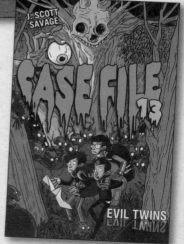